"There's something else," Max added

"I think I should make it plain that it's because of who you are that I'm offering you the job."

Jane said thoughtfully, "Well, I know who I am, of course, but what am I, from your point of view?"

"You are Miss Jane Calvert," Max began, turning to look at her. "Your family lived in this house, you grew up in this village, went to an expensive girls' school and, surprisingly, made a success of a business career in the city.

"You look exactly what you are," he went on, "and always have been—the product of a secure and privileged background, with supreme confidence in your own place in things."

Jane faced him fully. "Tell me something, Max. Are you ashamed of coming from Piper Flats?"

Catherine George was born in Wales and, following her marriage to an engineer, lived eight years in Brazil at a gold-mine site. It was an experience she would later draw upon for her books, when she and her husband returned to England. Now, her husband helps manage their household so that Catherine can devote more time to her writing. They have two children, a daughter and a son, who share their mother's love of language and the written word.

Books by Catherine George

HARLEQUIN ROMANCE

2535—RELUCTANT PARAGON
2571—DREAM OF MIDSUMMER
2720—DESIRABLE PROPERTY
2822—THE FOLLY OF LOVING
2924—MAN OF IRON
2942—THIS TIME ROUND
3081—CONSOLATION PRIZE

HARLEQUIN PRESENTS

1016—LOVE LIES SLEEPING
1065—TOUCH ME IN THE MORNING
1152—VILLAIN OF THE PIECE
1184—TRUE PARADISE
1225—LOVEKNOT
1255—EVER SINCE EDEN
1321—COME BACK TO ME

ARROGANT INTERLOPER
Catherine George

Harlequin Books

TORONTO • NEW YORK • LONDON
AMSTERDAM • PARIS • SYDNEY • HAMBURG
STOCKHOLM • ATHENS • TOKYO • MILAN

Original hardcover edition published in 1990
by Mills & Boon Limited

ISBN 0-373-03129-7

Harlequin Romance first edition June 1991

ARROGANT INTERLOPER

CHAPTER ONE

AS THE car sped towards sunset, like an arrow aimed
for the gold, a slipstream of air rushed through the open
windows, heady with clover and new-cut grass and less
romantic undertones of fertiliser. Jane inhaled it deeply,
her eyes half-closed against the glare as she noticed a jet
plane like a tiny black needle trailing its thread of flame
along the brilliant horizon. Distracted by it a moment
too long, she overshot the turning into Watery Lane,
and in a flurry of gear-changing she hauled on the
steering-wheel, not even seeing the cyclist approaching
in the opposite direction until it was almost too late.

Jane gave a screech of horror, treading frantically on
the brakes—but in vain. The bicycle made nerve-jangling
contact with the bonnet of the car, rocketing the cyclist
into the ditch in a sprawling heap.

Jane burst from the car and ran to fall on her knees
beside the man. 'Are you all right? Did I hurt you? I'm
so dreadfully sorry—I just didn't see you——'

To her vast relief her victim scrambled to his feet,
cursing as he dusted himself off. His sweat-soaked
tracksuit had torn at elbow and knee on the brambles
lining the ditch, but his hood had somehow managed to
stay in place, secured by a draw-string. What little of
the man's face was visible was obscured by black-lensed
aviator glasses and a film of perspiration, and, moreover,
was so crimson with fury that Jane backed away in alarm
as the man advanced on her with menace, rubbing his
elbow.

5

'What the hell were you playing at?' he roared. 'You could have killed me!'

Jane dug her heels in, shaking like a jelly inside, but every hackle rampant at the man's tone even though she knew perfectly well that he was very much in the right. 'I apologise,' she said stiffly. 'I was dazzled by the light and overshot the turning. Besides,' she added, 'I didn't expect to encounter anyone along here. This is a private road.'

'In which case, madam, a "no trespassing" sign might be more advisable than mowing down stray cyclists.' He motioned her aside brusquely. 'If you'd get out of the way I'd like to see if my bike still functions.'

Flushing, Jane helped him right the bicycle, which was a very expensive piece of machinery; a little scratched, but miraculously still in one piece. The man mopped his face with his sleeve, gave the cycle a quick inspection, then prepared to mount.

'Oh, but please,' Jane protested. 'I'm sure the bicycle would fit into the car if I fold the back seat down. Can't I give you a lift home? You must be shaken—perhaps you should see a doctor.'

The man gave a bark of laughter. 'I'd rather stick to my bike—it's safer! Thanks just the same.' He slung a long leg over the saddle and moved slowly away, wobbling a little before he gained speed. Just before he turned out of Watery Lane he halted, putting one foot to the ground as he turned to look at her.

'By the way,' he called. 'Just for future reference—we drive on the left round here.' He gave her a mocking salute and went racing round the corner out of sight.

Jane glared after him balefully, then got in the car, limp with reaction now that the incident was over. It was galling, too, to know that the blame was entirely hers. She cursed herself irritably. Normally she was such a careful driver. But tonight it had been wonderful to get out of the city. After the heat and traffic the countryside had looked so tranquil and welcoming in all its new May greenery, she'd just let her concentration lapse at exactly the wrong moment. Not, she admitted honestly, that her concentration had been very marvellous all the way to Wyndcome—and home.

She drove the remaining half-mile to Dower Cottage with exaggerated care, glad when the beloved thatched roof came into sight. She parked the car at the paddock gate, then heaved out her suitcase and went round the back to the kitchen door and let herself in.

'I'm here,' she called as she dumped her suitcase on the flagstoned floor. 'Mother?' She went into the hall to call upstairs, but the house was empty.

Jane went back to the kitchen to make tea, feeling rather deflated. She was, she found, badly in need of a cuddle and some comfort on more than one count, but her parent seemed to be nowhere around. Then, as Jane added milk to her mug of strong tea, she noticed the note taped to the refrigerator.

'Back about eight, darling. Lending a hand with the bun-fight for the playgroup. If hungry, forage. Love, Mother.'

Jane grinned. Few events in the village functioned without her mother's help.

Jane drank her tea, then took her suitcase up to the tiny bedroom which had been hers all her life. As always, the memorabilia of childhood in the cramped, familiar surroundings soothed and relaxed her, and she spent a long interval at the window, gazing out over fields which rolled away to the river in one direction, and in the other up towards the big old house in the distance which had once, long ago, been her mother's home. By the time she went downstairs again she felt a lot better as she began preparations for a cold supper from the salad ingredients and home-baked ham left in readiness in the refrigerator, and was in the act of whisking up a dressing when her mother arrived home.

Olivia Calvert was a thin woman, tall like her daughter, with humorous eyes of the same golden brown shade as her child. But her hair, unlike Jane's smooth honey-coloured bob, was dark and curly, streaked with white, and her eyebrows were thick and black and unplucked, in a face tanned by the hours she spent in her beloved garden. She held out her arms without a word and Jane flew into them, laying her head on her mother's shoulder with a sob of relief at the comfort of the familiar embrace.

'Hello, darling,' said Mrs Calvert, hugging her child. 'Had a bad day?'

Jane nodded, and stood back, smiling ruefully. 'A pig of a day. Burning all one's boats is a surprisingly exhausting exercise! In the space of a few hours I've left my job, my flat and my life in London all behind me, kicking myself every step of the way for being such a fool. And, of course, I didn't escape without a final furious phone call from Adrian, who is not adapting to his role of jilted bridegroom very happily, I'm afraid. And who can blame him?' she added with remorse.

Olivia Calvert contemplated her tall, guilt-flushed daughter, reminded, as always, of delicious edible things like sherry and honey and cream to describe Jane's eyes and hair and skin. Not beautiful exactly, Jane was possessed of a brightness and glow and an interest in life which gave her something her mother considered far preferable to mere beauty. Jane, the less troublesome of Olivia Calvert's two girls, had always been secretly the apple of her mother's eye; her baby, the afterthought, the child born ten years after the first, who had never given a moment's trouble of any kind, temperamentally, academically or socially. Until now.

'So Adrian's not taking your change of heart kindly,' said Olivia with sympathy.

'No. You might go so far as to say he's incensed. Largely,' added Jane sadly, 'because I've upset all his carefully mapped-out schedule—or so it seems from his general gist.'

'You've hurt him, Jane,' her mother reminded her. 'He's extremely fond of you.'

Jane heaved a great sigh. 'I know. And I'm fond of him. I hated having to hurt him like that.' She turned large, troubled eyes on her mother. 'But suddenly it hit me that "fond" isn't enough. I want to be wildly, passionately in love with the man I marry, and I want him to feel the same about me. Which, in essence, is why I called off the wedding.'

'Let's have some supper,' said Mrs Calvert briskly. 'Things always seem worse on an empty stomach. All I received at the "do" this evening was a glass of very indifferent sherry and a sausage on a toothpick. For which not even the Lord could make me truly thankful, I regret to say.'

Jane laughed unsteadily, and hugged her mother, then sat down at the table to enjoy the meal with an appetite only slightly impaired by the gloom of her present situation.

Although Mrs Calvert gave a humorous account of her evening Jane was less attentive than usual, inwardly still preoccupied with the mystery of why on earth she had ever contemplated marriage with Dr Adrian Fry, who was a very clever biochemist, and quite a nice man, but not the masterful lover wild horses wouldn't have made her admit she'd always dreamed about. She was twenty-six years old, intelligent, efficient at her job of assistant personnel officer of a large group of retail stores in London. She owned a car and a flat, had lots of friends, both male and female; so all in all it seemed rather astonishing that she'd ever said yes when Adrian proposed.

'I must have been mad,' she said musingly, interrupting her mother mid-sentence.

'On which particular occasion?'

'When I promised to marry Adrian in the first place.'

'I agree. The prospect of America must have seduced you.'

Jane looked up, startled. 'Don't you like him?'

'Yes. But I've never thought you were ideally suited to each other, darling.'

Jane digested this for a time as they ate, then began to explain slowly, as much to herself as to her mother, that lately doubts had begun to creep in about the type of relationship she was likely to enjoy with Adrian. 'That's the point, really. I began to realise that "enjoy" wasn't the word, but I hated having to admit that I'd made a mistake.' She smiled ruefully at her mother. 'And because my darling sister had two last-minute changes of heart almost at the altar steps, I suppose I jibbed at subjecting you to the same old routine over again. The Curse of the Calverts, they ought to call it.'

'Probably something to do with the birth sign you share. Blame it on New Year's Eve.'

Jane's eyebrows rose. 'What do you mean?'

Mrs Calvert's eyes twinkled. 'Darling, don't be obtuse. Both of you arrived nine months after New Year's Eve— the product of too much champagne at the annual revels!'

Jane gave a crow of laughter. 'You wicked old lady! I'd never thought of that.'

'Wicked I like; old lady I don't.'

'You may *feel* like twenty, but nevertheless you're sixty-seven, Mother dear, and I wish you'd slow down a bit. Take things easy now and again.'

'Nonsense. Time enough for that when I'm dead.'

Jane shuddered, reminded of her brush with the angry cyclist, and gave an account of the accident. Mrs Calvert, after startled questions about the well-being of Jane's victim, had no suggestions to offer about the man's identity, reverting quickly to her daughter's plans for the future now that Jane had come to such an abrupt full stop in her life.

'I'm pretty much at a loss,' said Jane, depressed. 'I've made rather a mess of things, haven't I? Incidentally, thanks a lot for seeing the rector and giving back the local presents. I've done all that in London, and Dad's sorting out the reception people.'

'He must be quite used to it by now,' said Mrs Calvert. 'It isn't as if it's the first time——' She caught Jane's eye and they both began to laugh again at the thought of Phillida. It had been George Calvert's opinion at one time that, if his elder daughter ever did make it down the aisle, it was likely to be the only shotgun wedding on record with the gun prodding the bride in the back rather than the bridegroom. But in the end Phillida had been married in the Scottish kirk where all the Rintouls of Kilvaraigh had been married for centuries, and had needed no shotgun, or any persuasion at all, to join her Alastair at the altar.

While Mrs Calvert went out into the warm dusk to water her bedding plants, Jane took stock of her situation and tried to decide what to do. Because Adrian had received an offer he couldn't refuse from a research institute in the States, he'd insisted that Jane marry him at once and go with him. Which was why, not without a great deal of soul-searching, she'd resigned from her job, given up her flat and more or less put an end to the way of life she'd enjoyed for several years. She slumped on the sofa, frowning into space as she wound a lock of bright hair around her finger, wondering what on earth she was going to do next.

'Right,' said Mrs Calvert briskly, coming in to join her. 'Have you any ideas on future policy?'

Jane turned preoccupied eyes on her mother. 'In a word, no. I'll need to look for another job, for a start. Is it all right if I stay here for a bit, Mother—until I sort something out?'

Mrs Calvert looked a little uncomfortable. 'You can, of course, darling, but actually there's a bit of a snag. I wasn't going to bother you with it before the wedding, but under the circumstances——'

'What sort of snag?' demanded Jane, frowning.

'I've got to move out of this place.'

Jane's jaw dropped. '*Move?* From here? But where? You—we—we've always lived here!'

'Yes, but now the lease has run out. I only ever held it at all, you know, as a favour because I was a Verney.'

Jane's eyes took on a militant gleam. 'Do you mean to say that this upstart who bought Verney House is turning you out in the snow?'

Olivia Calvert grinned. 'Not exactly. Not much snow in May, for one thing. And, to be fair, Dower Cottage has been his property ever since he bought Verney House, which must be over a year ago. But now, I gather, he needs it as a home for his caretaker.'

'Does he, indeed!' Jane sprang up and began prowling round the kitchen table. 'We'll see about that. I'm not having some money-grubbing property developer evicting my mother, believe me.'

'Darling, he's perfectly within his rights. The lease was up ages ago. And, to be fair, you can't lump him in with those unprincipled cowboys who throw concrete horrors up all over the place. His developments win prizes. And he's transformed Verney House from a mouldering ruin into something quite beautiful apparently, according to Betty Cook who plays the organ in church. Her daughter goes up to help clean the place.'

'I'm not interested in what he's doing to *his* little nest, Mother—only his intentions towards ours!' said Jane, pacing faster.

Olivia Calvert shrugged. 'The letter I received said something about alternative accommodation being found for me.'

'Where?' asked Jane scathingly. 'In an old people's home?'

'No! In the village somewhere. He's coming to see me next week.'

Jane stared at her mother, stunned. Everyone in the village knew about Max Brigstock, of course: the whizz-kid property developer, who combined philanthropy with making money. He was well known in the City, too. Or as much as he cared to be. He was reputedly a bit of a recluse, something of a mystery man.

'Why must it be Dower Cottage?' asked Jane in angry frustration.

Mrs Calvert shrugged. 'Apparently Mr Brigstock is away a lot. And with a house like his he needs a care-taker for security, and a house for the caretaker. After all, Dower Cottage is rather the willow cabin at his gate, isn't it? In the ideal location for controlling all the comings and goings.'

Jane ground her teeth impotently. 'I'm surprised he doesn't have barbed wire or an electrified fence. What's he got up there? The crown jewels?' She flung away to glare out of the window at the road which led to one-time Verney House. 'And now, I take it, you're sup-posed to pack your traps and trail off meekly to some hovel in the village just because this—this get-rich-quick upstart snaps his fingers!'

'Don't be melodramatic, darling.'

Jane wasn't listening. Her mind was still grappling with the unthinkable fact that Dower Cottage might no longer be there for her to run home to whenever she felt like it.

'Does Father know about this?' she asked after a while, brightening.

'No. It's nothing to do with him. As you know perfectly well, we're having one of our detached periods.' Mrs Calvert's face took on a familiar mulish look, and Jane sighed.

'He cares for you very much you know, Mother.'

'Possibly. But not enough to spend his life permanently here with me in Wyndcombe, remember. His muse, it seems, deserts him when subjected to a surfeit of country air.'

'Would you *like* him here permanently?' asked Jane with delicacy.

Olivia Calvert's smile was indulgent. 'We've had this conversation lots of times, Jane, and the answer's always the same. I've arranged my life to function remarkably well without George Calvert, RA, for the moment; and he quite obviously does the same without me, going by the success he's had lately. So do give up, darling. You're flogging a dead horse.'

'I thought he might be able to help. Beard your wicked landlord in his den and all that.'

'You are not to mention it to him.' Mrs Calvert caught her daughter's hand. 'Promise you won't say one word about this to your father.'

Jane bent to kiss her mother's tanned cheek. 'All right. I promise. If that's what you want.' She straightened, her eyes glinting. 'Incidentally Father, when I gave him the glad news, was not at all upset that I'd sent Adrian packing—his words, not mine, I hasten to add. On this one sole subject you are both in agreement, Mother.'

'Miracle of miracles!' Olivia laughed, then eyed her daughter quizzically. 'Now, before we drop the subject forever, tell me honestly, why did you say yes when Adrian proposed?'

'I thought it was about time that I started to think of settling down, having a family.' Jane gave her mother a wry little smile. 'And although I know lots of men, Mother, Adrian Fry's was the only proposal—of marriage anyway—that I've had in a long time!'

Jane woke next morning to a day bright with sunshine and glowered at it, feeling that it should have been raining cats and dogs in keeping with her mood—which had been low enough one way and another before she arrived home, without the added shock of hearing that the lease was up on Dower Cottage.

'Bad night?' asked her mother over breakfast.

'Fairly. About two in the morning I remembered I hadn't unpacked the car. Is it OK if I stow my excess luggage in Philly's old room?'

'Of course.' Mrs Calvert regarded her daughter's downcast face thoughtfully. 'Speaking of the car, I wonder if you'd mind doing a few errands for me this morning, darling. I promised some jumble for the sale at the church hall this afternoon, and Mrs Johnson at the shop is keeping me a nice fresh chicken for tomorrow's lunch——'

'Anything you say, Mother. Make a list.' Jane grinned. 'Therapy for miserable daughters, I take it—keep 'em busy.'

'Something like that. It's also a fairly long trek into the village, on foot with a bin-bag of cast-offs, for an ageing body like me,' added Mrs Calvert, with a melodramatic quaver in her voice.

Jane laughed and went off to unpack the car, then tidied herself up and started out to do her mother's errands. The visit to the village shop proved very interesting. Without volunteering a word about the move from Dower Cottage Jane learned that it was not the only place in the neighbourhood to be vacated at Max Brigstock's behest. On the far boundary of his estate the Briggs family had recently been obliged to move from Verney Lodge into a cottage in Wyndcombe itself. The Lodge was needed for unspecified private purposes, was the mysterious comment. Jane was seething as she bore her mother's groceries back to the car. Mr Max Brigstock, it seemed, was bent on something of a purge. Quite the wicked landlord, she thought angrily—but one who had another think coming when it came to Jane Calvert's mother, even if he didn't know it yet.

Jane's resentment mounted as she drove back to Dower Cottage. So much so that, when she came in sight of it, she was seized by a sudden impulse and drove past the cottage along the private road which mounted steeply until it ended at the newly painted gates of what had once been Verney House. Since the gates stood open Jane drove on through parkland which looked incredibly immaculate; very different from the previous time she'd seen it. Everywhere she looked there were signs of care and attention: grass clipped, trees expertly lopped, not a pot-hole in sight in the driveway leading up to the beautiful building which now went by the name of Phoenix House.

As she parked the car on the gravelled apron in front of it, Jane examined the house with eyes prepared to be hostile as she searched for brash new changes. But her belligerence subsided a little as she looked in vain. Try as she might she could find no fault with the restoration, which had been made with such skill and care for the original construction it was hard to believe that, only a year or so ago, the place had been falling into such disrepair that she had doubted it could ever be put right again. Yet the rosy brickwork looked for all the world as though it had always been just the way it was now:

a beautiful, weathered frame for the windows which glittered intact in the noon sunlight. Jane bit her lip, seized by sudden qualms about bearding the lion in his den, a bit chary now of marching right up to his imposing front door. She skirted the conservatory and went round to the back of the house instead, where she found a young woman feeding a trio of kittens in the sunshine outside the kitchens.

'Good morning,' said Jane, and smiled. 'I wondered if I might have a word with Mr Brigstock.'

The woman looked taken aback. 'Did you ring? I'm sorry, I didn't hear the doorbell.'

Jane flushed. 'I didn't, actually. I just came straight round here.'

'Oh, I see.' A pair of bright dark eyes regarded Jane steadily for a moment. 'It's Miss Calvert, isn't it?'

Jane smiled, surprised. 'Why, yes.'

'You're not a reporter these days, by any chance, Miss Calvert?'

'No, indeed. I just want a word on a personal matter.'

The woman hesitated, then shrugged. 'I suppose it'll be all right for *you* to see him. He's in what used to be the walled garden. You'll know the way, of course. I'd come with you, only I've got a cake due out of the oven any minute.'

Jane thanked her and walked away quickly in the direction of the walled garden, which she remembered as a dilapidated place full of ruined old glasshouses and neglected fruit trees espaliered against warm, south-facing brick walls. As she crunched along freshly gravelled paths Jane saw that the old walls she remembered so well had been repaired with the same loving hand as the house, and a stone archway now marked the opening to the vegetable garden.

Jane squared her shoulders as she passed under the arch, pausing in surprise at the scene which greeted her.

Previously the place had been littered with smashed glass
and weeds and bricks and stones, but now all was smooth
green turf, interspersed here and there with flowering
shrubs and small ornamental trees. The espaliered fruit
trees were still there, or others just like them, in sym-
metrical tracery against the mellow brick of three of the
walls. But the far wall had been removed. Now one could
see straight into the sunken Italian garden. Only it wasn't
a sunken garden any more. It was a pool which glittered
in the sun in a setting of natural stone—and in the pool
a man cut through the water in a powerful crawl.

Jane gritted her teeth as she walked towards the pool,
ignoring a sudden traitorous longing to turn tail and run.
Now she was here she would do exactly what she'd come
here to do. The man swam on, powering through the
water with effortless strokes, unaware of the girl advancing towards him across the grass. Jane felt suddenly
very warm. She knew that her colour was high, and
wished she could have stayed cool and remote to gain
the advantage she needed. And something more stunning
in the way of clothes would have been nice too, she
thought, swallowing, now that an impulse had brought
her to confront Mr Brigstock of Phoenix House. Instead
she was wearing the sort of thing she always wore at
home in summer: flat comfortable shoes in well-polished
leather, a long cotton skirt in a rose print and a plain
pink shirt with the sleeves rolled up.

Jane came to a halt and stood at the edge of the pool,
watching the man race away from her unaware that he
was being observed; a moment later he heaved himself
out of the pool to reach for a terry-cloth robe thrown
across one of the wicker chairs ranged about. Her eyes
widened in dismay as she realised there was something
familiar about him. As he tied the robe he turned suddenly, his eyes narrowing as he caught sight of the girl

looking at him down the length of the pool. He strode
towards her, mopping at his hair with a towelling sleeve.

Jane wished the ground would open up and swallow
her as she recognised the man she'd knocked off his cycle
the evening before. This time his face was revealed to
Jane in every detail: ruler-straight black brows, a Roman
nose, wide uncompromising mouth above a pugnacious
jaw in need of a shave. The eyes assessing Jane were
unexpected in that swarthy face: a bright, green-flecked
hazel, with a hard, metallic gleam in them which did
nothing at all to calm the butterflies in her stomach.

'Forgive me for intruding,' she began, knowing from
the start that her mission was doomed. 'My name is
Calvert—Jane Calvert. My mother lives in Dower
Cottage.'

'So you're Jane Calvert,' he said slowly, in the hard,
resolute voice she had taken such exception to the evening
before. 'I'm Max Brigstock, the chap you mowed down
last night. Do I take it you've come to apologise?'

Jane's flush deepened, and for a moment she was
tempted to lie and say yes. She shook her head. 'I won't
pretend that's my reason for coming here. For one thing
I had no idea who you were, Mr Brigstock. Otherwise
perhaps I might have done.'

'But only perhaps.' One of the straight black brows
lifted.

Jane decided that retreat was the only thing possible.
Now that she'd actually met Max Brigstock face to face—
for the second time, unfortunately—there was no hope
at all for the favour she had been about to ask. Not even
ask, she remembered, quailing a little. Only a few
minutes before she had been prepared to demand, not
request. But something in the way this man was looking
at her was stripping her of every last little scrap of poise
she possessed. She pulled herself together hurriedly.

'I really shouldn't have come here,' she said, meeting the metallic gleam head-on. 'But at least it gives me the opportunity to apologise for my carelessness yesterday evening, Mr Brigstock. I'm relieved to know that you weren't hurt. Now I must be going.'

'Not before I find out why you've come,' he said curtly, and held one of the cane chairs for her. 'If your motive isn't apology you must have some other reason for wanting to see me.'

Wishing she was a million miles away, Jane sat down as, with perfect timing, the woman she'd spoken to earlier came towards them carrying a tray of coffee. Max Brigstock took the tray with a brief word of thanks; the young woman smiled at Jane then went away again, leaving an awkward silence behind her which Jane's host broke at last by asking her to pour.

Jane did so reluctantly, noting the quality of the very beautiful cups. Crown Derby, with fluted edges, and very thin. Not at all the sort of china she would have expected.

The owner of Phoenix House and, more relevantly to Jane, owner of Dower Cottage, sat drinking coffee in silence, his eyes fixed on Jane's flushed, tense face as he waited for her to speak.

Jane sat with her eyes on her cup, trying to frame the words that she had intended to hurl at him with such scorn. But now she was actually in Max Brigstock's presence it wasn't nearly so easy. For one thing he was not only years younger, but a great deal more physically attractive, than she had expected. In her mind she'd conjured up a picture of a hard-bitten middle-aged tycoon. Instead she was confronted with a muscular male specimen not all that many years older than herself. She would have felt more at ease too, she thought unhappily, if he'd been fully dressed. The sight of his long bare legs wasn't helping her at all with the matter in hand. And since it was obvious that the man watching her so intently had no intention of making things easier for her Jane had no option, at last, but to say her piece.

'Mr Brigstock,' she began with a rush, 'the reason I'm here is to ask you not to turn my mother out of Dower Cottage.'

The hard eyes flickered for an instant, the straight brows knitting together in a discouraging scowl. 'Turn your mother *out*? What are you talking about?'

Jane's chin lifted aggressively. 'I can't expect you to understand, of course——'

'Why not? Do you consider my intellect insufficient to grasp whatever you have to say?'

Jane went scarlet. 'No! No, of course not. I merely meant that it wasn't quite the same for the Briggs family—they'd only lived in the Lodge for a year or two. But for my mother—for me—it's different. After all, you're a newcomer to these parts, so naturally I can't expect you to realise what it would mean for my mother to have to leave the place that's been home to her since before her marriage.' Jane looked at him imploringly. 'Mr Brigstock, isn't it possible for you to renew her lease on the cottage—find some other accommodation for your caretaker?'

Max Brigstock's swarthy face wore a very odd expression, rather as though he couldn't believe what he was hearing. 'Miss Calvert, did your mother send you here today?'

'Absolutely not!' Jane grimaced. 'She'll give me a frightful dressing down when she knows, believe me.' She tried to smile at his unresponsive face. 'I just thought——'

'You just thought that, although I've apparently turned the Briggs family out of the Lodge into the street, lock stock and barrel, with the eviction of an elderly lady for an encore, I might be persuaded to change my mind if I was asked very nicely by a younger lady prepared to use her looks and sex to divert me from my villainous course.'

He spoke with such lack of inflection that Jane could hardly believe what she was hearing for a moment.

'I'm sorry you find it so amusing,' she said tightly, and jumped to her feet.

Max Brigstock followed suit in a more leisurely manner, and stood with his arms folded across his chest. 'On the contrary; I don't find it in the least amusing,' he said coldly.

'I'm obviously wasting my time—and yours. So sorry to have troubled you, Mr Brigstock.' Jane turned on her heel, prepared for flight, but his voice stayed her.

'Hold your horses, Miss Calvert. You can't just barge in here and make accusations like that. I suggest you get the facts straight.'

Unwillingly Jane turned to face him again, her eyes drawn involuntarily to the man's tanned, muscular legs below the thigh-length hem of his robe. She looked away in a hurry, conscious of the sardonic gleam in his eyes which told her that he knew exactly why she was so hot under her crisp pink collar.

'From information given to me,' said Max Brigstock, rather with the air of one addressing a meeting, 'I gather your mother is a lady much given to good works in Wyndcombe.'

Jane frowned suspiciously. 'Yes. She was Miss Verney of Verney House at one time——'

'I'm well aware of your pedigree, Miss Calvert!'

'You mistake my meaning, Mr Brigstock,' retorted Jane. 'I was merely trying to point out that my mother was brought up in the habit of visiting the old and ill and needy.'

'Exactly. Now, apropos of this, I believe Mrs Calvert is said to be in her late sixties——'

'Which doesn't qualify her for removal to an old people's home!'

Max Brigstock looked dangerous for a moment, his mouth clamped together in a rigid line. 'What I'm trying to point out, if you'd be so good as to let me do so without interruption, is that the mile and a half into Wyndcombe for whatever errand of mercy Mrs Calvert is employed in is a fair trek for her. I gather she doesn't drive.'

Jane's eyes flickered slightly. 'She—she would never learn. She *enjoys* walking.'

'Are you quite sure of that? Even in winter when the weather's bad?' He let that point sink in, then said smoothly, 'Perhaps your mother mentioned that alternative accommodation would be found for her.'

'Well, yes,' admitted Jane reluctantly, her eyes resentful. 'But nothing was said about where.'

'There are two properties up for sale in the village itself at the moment. Your mother's welcome to view them at any time convenient to her.'

'Nothing I can say will change your mind about Dower Cottage, then?' Jane said bleakly.

Max Brigstock surveyed her hostile face for a moment in silence. 'No, Miss Calvert. On the other hand perhaps I should make it clear that your mother may choose either of the two alternatives I have in mind, and live at either one for the same rent she now pays for Dower Cottage.'

Jane frowned at him suspiciously. She knew quite well that the rent her mother paid was in no way realistic. It had risen hardly at all over the past few years, despite the soaring property market.

'I don't understand,' she said uncertainly.

'I don't expect you to, Miss Calvert. Nor do I feel the need to explain. After all, this is your mother's home we're discussing. You, I believe, left Wyndcombe for London years ago.'

'Even so, I still regard the cottage as my home! But then, I don't really expect *you* to understand, either, Mr Brigstock. I apologise for taking up so much of your valuable time.'

'Yes,' he agreed, glancing at the Rolex Oyster on his wrist. 'I'm afraid I'll have to ask you to excuse me, Miss Calvert. I'm expecting some people for a meeting any minute now.'

'On a Saturday?' said Jane involuntarily.

He gave her a patronising smile. 'People like me actually work now and then on Saturdays, you know. It's the way we make money to buy the property we turn elderly ladies out of.'

Controlling the urge to connect her fist with his dark-shadowed jaw, Jane inclined her head graciously. 'Thank you so much for the coffee, Mr Brigstock. Good morning.'

'I'll take you back to your car.'

'Oh, no, please, I wouldn't *dream* of troubling you. I know the way perfectly well. I've had the run of the gardens all my life, you know. Up to now.' Jane gave him a smile as sweet and cold as a vanilla ice, then walked away across the grass, forcing herself to take her time, certain that Max Brigstock's bright, cold eyes were following her until she was through the archway and out of range of his twenty-twenty vision.

CHAPTER TWO

OLIVIA CALVERT was deeply displeased when she heard where Jane had been; even more so when she learned the motive for the visit. Jane knew very well that a sharp tongue-lashing would have been her fate at any other time, but Mrs Calvert contented herself by producing coals of fire in the shape of the letter which had arrived that morning, while Jane was out.

It was on paper headed 'Phoenix House, Wyndcombe', and Jane's heart plummeted as she read that the houses Max Brigstock had in mind as possible choices for her mother's future home were far from being the hovels of her own scathing description. Both properties were larger than Dower Cottage, and conveniently situated in Wyndcombe village itself. Appointments to view could be arranged for Mrs Calvert early the following week at any time convenient to her.

Jane groaned and put the letter down, feeling an utter fool. 'All right—say it. Tell me I'm an impulsive moron.'

'Darling, you've always loved this place so passionately I suppose I can't blame you for chancing your luck with Mr Brigstock.' Mrs Calvert looked a little guilty. 'But you know, Jane, I must confess I quite fancy living right in the village. It's getting a bit much at my age to have to hike so far to everything, or bring someone out of their way for a lift home.'

Jane eyed her mother challengingly. 'You might have put me right on all this last night!'

'You were in a bit of a state last night, Jane. I didn't think it was the time to say that I actually *wanted* out of the cottage. Mind you,' Mrs Calvert added drily, 'if I'd thought for one moment that you'd go barging in on our new neighbour like that, I'd have said so in words of one syllable.'

Jane's mood deteriorated even further when she was informed that the Briggs family, far from being unhappy at their move, were delighted with their new home, which was far more modern and conveniently situated for the shops and village school than the old one.

'I should have thought, Jane,' said Mrs Calvert severely, 'that you'd have made completely sure of your facts before making such a cake of yourself with Mr Brigstock.'

Jane agreed glumly, vowing never to give in to impulse again.

'Daisy Whitehead's asked us to supper, by the way,' said Mrs Calvert over lunch.

Jane groaned. 'Oh, no! Please say you refused! You know I adore the Whiteheads, but under the circumstances——'

'I said we'd go.' Mrs Calvert handed her daughter a mug of coffee. 'No point in sulking in our tent. Daisy says brooding's bad for you, Jane, and I agree. She'll expect us at eight.'

The Whiteheads were Olivia Calvert's oldest friends, and very fond of Jane, their godchild. Normally Jane would have been delighted at the prospect of an evening at their house, where the food was always wonderful and the conversation lively. But tonight she would have preferred an evening alone to lick her wounds, one way and another, particularly after the hideous embarrassment of the morning. What a fool she'd been, she thought despairingly as she dressed, rushing in like a bull in a china shop to persuade Max Brigstock against a course of action her mother was all for, anyway.

'Do you feel too tired to walk, Mother?' she asked, when she was ready.

'No, darling, of course not. It's a lovely night.' Olivia Calvert smiled. 'You fancy having a drink, I gather.'

'For once, I do. I need some Dutch courage. So no driving.'

'Very sensible. I like that dress. Is it new?'

Jane gave a twirl. 'It should have been off to America next week, but as it's not I thought I'd give it an airing tonight.'

'Lovely colour, darling.'

Jane smoothed a hand over the thin silk absently. 'Rather like the brick up at the house, actually. You know, the upstart's done a good job on the place, grieve me though it does to admit it. Will I do, then?' she added, smiling.

Mrs Calvert touched a loving hand to her daughter's cheek. 'Yes, Jane, you'll do. Admirably—now and always. Only stop calling Mr Brigstock "the upstart".'

The sun was setting as they walked along the quiet road. Doves were cooing somewhere close at hand, there was an occasional bleat from the sheep grazing in a nearby field, and the peace of it all did wonders for nerves sorely tried by recent events. Jane was glad, she found, now that the initial effort had been made, that her mother had accepted this evening's invitation.

'I expect they'll be out on the lawn as usual, in weather like this,' said Olivia Calvert as they arrived. 'Let's go straight round to the back garden.'

Daisy Whitehead was the same age as Olivia, but otherwise she was as different from her friend as it was possible to be: small, bouncy, with a mop of white curls which gave her the look of an elderly cherub. At the sight of her visitors she sprang out of her garden chair with an agility many a younger woman would have envied, her arms outstretched to Jane.

'Darling! How are you coping? Did your young man make a ghastly fuss? Are you terribly upset about it all?'

Jane hugged her godmother close. 'Hello, Aunt Daisy. Yes to the first two, and quite a bit to the last. But I'll get over it. So will Adrian.'

'Where's Ben?' asked Olivia, subsiding into a deck-chair with a sigh of content.

'He went down to the off-licence for some cigars, but not before he concocted a jug of deliciously decadent champagne cocktail!' Daisy dashed into the house, and Jane curled up on a rug, leaning her head back against her mother's knee, feeling better than she had all day.

'All right, love?' asked Mrs Calvert quietly.

'Yes. Surprisingly so, really, I ought to be racked with guilt, and all that.'

'Which you are, only you're putting a good face on it.'

'Stop mind-reading, you perceptive woman.' Jane twisted round to grin up at her mother. 'You were right to bring me here tonight. Not much use crying over spilt milk at home when we can drink champagne cocktails here!'

'I hope you like them,' cried Daisy, reappearing with a tall, frosted jug. 'It was to have been a little pre-wedding party for you tonight, Jane, but we cancelled when—well, you know. Nevertheless Ben thought the champagne cocktails were a good idea under the cir-cumstances,' she said, smiling at Jane as she poured out.

Jane thanked her gratefully, apologising for the trouble she was causing everyone, then tasted her drink with re-spect. 'A good idea under any circumstances! If this is champagne cocktail, I love it. Sounds too sophisticated and Noel Cowardly for words!'

The other two laughed, and Daisy stroked Jane's hair fondly before settling down beside her friend. 'People are so dull these days—all they ever seem to drink are

G and Ts, whereas in our youth we drank White Ladies and Sidecars and——'

'*You* may have done, Daisy,' interrupted Olivia, laughing. 'I was rarely given the chance!'

'Nonsense, Liv—oh, there's Ben...' Daisy Whitehead halted, looking horrified as she saw that her large husband was not alone. 'Oh, my goodness, I thought...' She threw a look of desperate entreaty at Jane and Olivia as Ben Whitehead shepherded his companion across the grass towards them.

'Hello, Olivia, and Jane, my pet, gorgeous as ever. Daisy, sorry I was so long.' Ben gave his wife a look which spoke volumes. 'I met up with Brigstock here just as he was arriving.'

Max Brigstock's face wore a guarded look as he shook Daisy's hand. 'How do you do, Mrs Whitehead. It was very kind of you to invite me tonight. I hope I'm not too early.'

Daisy smiled brightly at him. 'No, no! Not in the least. How nice to meet you. I've heard so much...' She remembered some of the things she'd heard and changed the subject hastily. 'Do let me introduce you. Olivia Calvert and her daughter, Jane, who's our godchild, you know. Mr Max Brigstock, darlings.'

Jane was on her feet, hoping that her smile was adequate disguise for her horror in coming face to face with her adversary of the morning again.

'Miss Calvert and I have already met,' said Max Brigstock who, judging by his poker face, was plainly no more delighted than Jane. 'You could say we ran into each other last night.' He turned to Olivia. 'How do you do, Mrs Calvert? We know each other in a way too, of course, but only by letter.'

'I'm very glad to meet you in person,' said Olivia Calvert, who was regarding the tall, dark newcomer with a thoughtful expression in her eyes. 'But haven't we met before somewhere, Mr Brigstock?'

He shook his head. 'I don't think so. I've been away from the district for the past few years. I returned from the States only a day or two ago.'

Mrs Calvert laughed. 'In which case you must have wished you hadn't. Allow me to say how relieved I am to see you in one piece. Jane ran him down on his bicycle last night on her way home from London,' she added for the Whiteheads' benefit.

Daisy frankly goggled. 'On your *bicycle*, Mr Brigstock?'

The swarthy face remained politely blank. 'It's one of the ways I try to keep fit. When I'm down here I cycle and swim a lot. In the City I work out at a gym.' His hard eyes turned in Jane's direction, lingering slightly on her shuttered face. 'Unfortunately Miss Calvert and I chose to turn a corner simultaneously in opposite directions last night, and I landed in the ditch.'

Ben Whitehead guffawed. 'Good job it was Jane. She's a jolly good driver. If it had been her sister Phillida you probably wouldn't be here to tell the tale! Now,' he added briskly, 'what'll you have? The girls are on champagne cocktails, but I can offer you something a bit more sustaining, if you'd prefer.' He caught his wife's eye and added, 'Perhaps you might like to take a stroll along my little stretch of river here while we enjoy it.'

Jane returned to her rug at her mother's feet as, glasses in hand, the two men strolled out of sight, and Daisy collapsed on the chair beside Olivia with an explosive sigh.

'Oh, darlings, what can I say? Mr Brigstock gave Ben a lift home one day in that rather splendid car of his, so Ben invited him for tonight, never dreaming he'd accept because he's known to be a bit of a recluse. Only he did accept. Then both of us thought that the other one had let him know it was off.' Her blue eyes gazed beseechingly at Jane. 'Do say you forgive us, darling. We must be getting old.'

Jane smiled stoically. 'Nonsense, Aunt Daisy. You'll never be old. And I won't be rude to him, I promise.'

'I never thought for a moment you would, darling,' said Daisy, astonished. 'I meant, I'm sorry if it's difficult for you under the circumstances.'

Mrs Calvert explained about Jane's ill-fated visit to Phoenix House earlier that day, in an effort to avoid pitfalls over dinner in company with a guest who for Jane, if no one else, was extremely unwelcome.

'Such a good thing we're eating salmon,' said Daisy thankfully, and sprang to her feet as she heard the men returning. 'Keep the conversation going, Liv, while I pop inside and see to the meal.'

Daisy Whitehead was an accomplished hostess. Soon they were eating the sort of simple, perfect meal she produced with such seeming lack of effort that no one would have guessed that the table had been hastily laid with another place, and that the meal had been intended for four people instead of five. She'd seated Max Brigstock between herself and Olivia at the table, with Ben and Jane facing them, and was in her element as she questioned him about the work he'd been doing on Verney House.

'Only I must learn to call it Phoenix House now, of course,' she said, apologetically. 'It's just that it belonged to Olivia's family at one time and it's hard to get used to the different name.'

'Why Phoenix, Mr Brigstock?' enquired Olivia Calvert, as she spread Daisy's famous garlicky liver pâté on a curl of Melba toast.

Jane detected a flicker of animation on Max Brigstock's face as he explained that, although the old house had not actually burned down, the new name seemed appropriate for the house that he'd created from the remains, if not the ashes, of the old one.

'A bit poetic, I suppose, for a man who had to leave school before his A-levels,' he added, looking up to meet Jane's unsmiling gaze. 'But as my name isn't Verney I didn't feel entitled to use it.'

'You could have, and welcome,' Mrs Calvert told him affably. 'There's only me left now. And I would have been only too pleased.'

'That's very kind of you, Mrs Calvert.' His answering smile held irony. 'But you're in a minority. I don't think people in the village approved of its being Verney House once I'd bought it.'

'They were probably afraid you'd knock it down and build houses all over the site,' remarked Jane, winning a frown of disapproval from her mother.

'Whereas I simply wanted a home here,' he said stiffly.

'Here in Wyndcombe, or simply the country?' asked Olivia with interest.

'Here in Wyndcombe, Mrs Calvert.'

'Why here particularly?' Jane couldn't help asking.

Max looked across at her through the flickering candlelight. 'I have my reasons.'

Rebuffed, Jane turned deliberately to Ben Whitehead, questioning him about the weight of the magnificent salmon Daisy set on the table for the next course, while Mrs Calvert plunged into a discussion on the improvements her dinner partner had made in the gardens of his new home.

Ben Whitehead proposed a toast. 'Welcome to Wyndcombe, Brigstock.'

Max Brigstock's face lost its guarded expression for an instant. 'Thank you. Thank you very much. You're very kind.' He raised his own glass. 'And may I propose a toast in turn. To Miss Calvert—to the happy bride.'

Jane stared at him, horrified, while the other three sat momentarily dumb.

Max Brigstock looked from one face to another, frowning. 'I've obviously said something wrong.'

Mrs Calvert cleared her throat. 'You weren't to know. Please don't be embarrassed. You were quite right in thinking that Jane *was* to have been married next Saturday, but she—she's changed her mind. The wedding has been cancelled.'

Max Brigstock looked frankly appalled as he stared across at Jane, who sat like a statue—except that no statue ever had such flushed cheeks. This was only the third encounter she'd ever had with Max Brigstock, Jane thought bitterly, yet every time they met she found herself either losing her temper or wanting to run away and hide. Like now. And on none of the occasions had the fault been in any way his, which made it all the more galling.

'I apologise for embarrassing you, Miss Calvert,' he said formally, and she forced herself to smile.

'I'm sure you're more embarrassed than we are. Please think nothing of it. As my mother said, you had no way of knowing.' She turned to her godparents with a determined smile. 'This salmon is quite wonderful, by the way.'

Daisy Whitehead took her cue effortlessly, doing her utmost to draw her unexpected guest into the conversation at all opportunities. And gradually Max Brigstock began to respond, thawing a little in the warmth shown him by everyone bar Jane.

Jane's friendly instincts, however, were temporarily in abeyance. She sat in silence for the most part, her attention on her plate as she ate her salmon and drank her wine, determined not to let the incident affect her enjoyment of the meal. As they moved on to an iced praline soufflé and the cheese Daisy produced to accompany it, Jane decided that it was time to make a contribution to the conversation unless she fancied a severe reprimand from her mother when she got home.

'Do you think you'll enjoy living in this part of the world, Mr Brigstock?' she asked when there was a lull. 'Is Wyndcombe new to you?'

He applied ripe Stilton to a Bath Oliver with concentration. 'No, to the last part,' he said slowly, his eyes rising from his task to meet hers. 'When I was a child I lived not too far away from here at Pipers Flats, the cottages near the sawmill. As for the rest, I'm not sure yet whether I'll enjoy living in this part of the world or not. I didn't much when I was a child. I'm hoping for better things this time.'

It was Jane's turn to feel nonplussed. Her superficial, almost perfunctory questions had brought a response rather unwelcome in its detail. To herself, at least. The others were deeply interested, unaffected and natural in their curiosity about the boy who'd made the transition from the slums around Pipers Mill to his present entrepreneurial eminence. It was plain that Max Brigstock, after the initial piece of information, had little taste for discussing his past, but felt obliged to sing for his supper by telling his hosts a few unembroidered details about the childhood spent with grandparents before he left school in his teens and went away to London.

'Where I worked by day and studied for A-levels in the evenings and weekends.' Max Brigstock smiled slightly. 'I just went on from there,' he said simply, as though it explained everything.

The three older people made no bones about showing how impressed they were, but Jane remained withdrawn. If tonight had been intended as a diversion to take her mind off the cancelled wedding it had been quite a success in one way, she reflected wryly. But as they lingered over coffee in the candlelit room she studied Max Brigstock covertly, wondering what went on behind that carefully blank exterior. He dressed well enough, she admitted reluctantly. Unlike on their previous encounters, he was conventionally attired in a lightweight grey flannel suit with a crisp white shirt and sober silk tie. His hair, now that she was seeing it for the first time under normal circumstances, waved slightly, and was glossy and very dark, in a Celtic rather than a Latin way. And she knew there were impressive muscles under that expensive cloth too, having seen them first-hand this morning while he was tearing up and down his new pool like a barracuda. All in all, no one could deny that Max Brigstock was a very attractive man, with a keen, intelligent look to his face that would have been very much to Jane's taste had he been almost any other man in the world.

Jane came to with a start to find the object of her scrutiny looking at her across the table, eyebrows raised.

Olivia Calvert frowned at her, and Jane bit her lip.

'I'm so sorry, Mr Brigstock. Did you ask me something? I was miles away.'

'I merely asked if you were staying in Wyndcombe long,' he said, patently regretting now that he'd bothered to say anything at all.

'Indefinitely, until I get another job. I've just resigned from my present one—given up my flat, too,' she said with frank regret.

'You hadn't planned to work after your marriage, then?'

Jane shrugged. 'Indeed I had. But my intention was to find something in Boston—Massachusetts, not Lincolnshire. That's where Adrian, my—my former fiancé, is about to take up a research post.'

'So you're out of a job.'

'Yes. But not for long, hopefully.' Jane caught her mother's eye. 'I'm sorry to interrupt, Mother, but would you mind if we started back now? I'm beginning to flag.'

Out of the corner of her eye she saw Max Brigstock's face set in hard lines, as if he'd taken offence because she'd put an end to their conversation, and she decided that his company was rather wearing for someone in her present fragile frame of mind.

Wearing or not, Jane found that she had to put up with his company a while longer before she could escape since, after farewells had been made to the Whiteheads, Max Brigstock insisted on escorting the Calverts home. He walked between the two women, his head bent towards Olivia as he mentioned the pool he'd had built in what had been the sunken garden in her youth.

'You're lucky to have weather warm enough to swim in it at the moment,' said Jane, feeling she ought to make some kind of comment.

'I'm thinking of enclosing it so that I can swim in winter,' he answered, and Olivia laughed.

'You're making Jane envious. She loves swimming.'

There was a pause.

'You're welcome to use the pool at any time, of course, Miss Calvert,' said Max Brigstock distantly.

'How kind,' she answered, privately making a vow never to set foot inside the gates of Phoenix House again, let alone dabble her toes in its private pool.

Olivia Calvert invited their escort in when they arrived at Dower Cottage but he refused, taking his leave with punctilious courtesy, obviously in a hurry to escape.

'Was it necessary to be quite so hostile, Jane!' Mrs Calvert asked as she went into the kitchen to make tea.

'I'm not a saint, Mother. I went to Daisy's under protest because you thought it would be good for me, and then, for my sins, had to endure an evening with the man who was so—so——'

'Honest?' came a voice from the kitchen.

'No! He wasn't just *honest* this morning. He was damned insulting.' Jane scowled at her toes as she kicked off her high-heeled sandals. 'Anyway, just whose side are you on, Mother?'

'If there *are* sides I'm on yours, Jane, every time,' said Mrs Calvert, returning with two mugs of tea.

Jane smiled gratefully. 'In that case, because you're such a perfect mother, I'll give you my answerphone as a reward. You'll enjoy knowing who rang while you're out whooping it up at the Mothers' Union.'

'My, my, we *are* in a snide mood!' Mrs Calvert thrust a cup of tea in her daughter's hand. 'I don't think champagne cocktails can be good for your disposition, my girl. You hardly spoke a word all evening—and when you did you weren't exactly the spirit of goodwill.'

Jane pulled a face. 'Sorry. It was the shock of seeing the upstart appear out of the blue like that.'

'Stop calling him that, child.'

'But that's exactly what he is—to me. You should see it all up there at the house—everything so polished and perfect.' Jane's eyes narrowed. 'I'm jolly sure the boy from Pipers Flats wouldn't have dreamed of doing all that somewhere else. I bet you any money it was Verney House he had his heart set on from the moment he earned his first week's pay.'

'Then I take my hat off to him!'

'The more I think of it,' went on Jane, 'the more I'm certain that he wants to get his own back in some way on someone—possibly everyone—here for his unhappy childhood.'

'Surely not! Anyway, one thing you can't fault him for, Jane, is his frankness about his humble origins.'

'Very true. He practically rammed them down our throats!' Jane sat up suddenly. 'By the way, was tonight the first time he'd been asked anywhere locally?'

Olivia Calvert looked thoughtful. 'Well—yes, I suppose it must be. In general I think people in the village feel rather put off by the poor man's wealth, so to speak.'

'Doesn't *anyone* remember him as a child?'

Mrs Calvert shook her head, frowning. 'If they do, no one's said so. But you know, Jane, there's something so familiar about him—it keeps on eluding me. Tantalising.'

Jane gave an odd little smile. '*I* certainly haven't met the man before, to my knowledge. I'd know if I had. I don't like Mr Max Brigstock, but I won't deny that his particular brand of personality and looks come into the ''once seen, never forgotten'' category.'

CHAPTER THREE

NEXT morning Mrs Calvert proposed that they both go to morning service. Jane looked up from the Sunday paper in horror.

'You're not serious, Mother!'

'I certainly am. Let's run the gauntlet all in one. A lovely day like this usually brings a good turnout.'

Jane groaned. 'You're a cruel, harsh woman. But you're right, I suppose. Might as well get it over with.'

In actual fact morning service proved to be less of an ordeal than expected. With quite touching delicacy not a soul commented on the cancelled wedding when the Calverts came out of church. Consequently Jane was able to enjoy the walk home afterwards, right up until the moment they reached Watery Lane and a gleaming Aston Martin rounded the corner from the main road to purr to a halt beside them. Max Brigstock leaned from the window, looking hot and windblown behind familiar dark glasses.

'Good afternoon. You've obviously been to church.'

'We have indeed. Hello, Mr Brigstock.' Olivia Calvert smiled at him warmly.

His answering smile was a flash of white in his dark face. 'I shall be down here for most of the week. I wonder if I might call in fairly soon to discuss the houses I mentioned? The estate agent is fending other people off until you look them over.'

'Ah—then in that case, come for a drink tomorrow evening,' said Mrs Calvert promptly. 'Are you taking a holiday?'

'Afraid not—quite the opposite. I'm heavily involved in a project in this part of the world for the time being. I've been up to town this morning to collect some papers.'

'London and back before noon?'

'I left at first light. Best part of the day.' Max Brigstock glanced at Jane's unresponsive face. 'I'll come down about six-thirty tomorrow, then. Goodbye.'

The car moved off and Jane went into the house before it was out of sight, in a thoroughly bad mood again.

'I almost asked him to lunch,' said Mrs Calvert, eyeing her as she took off her hat, 'but something in your face told me it would not be a good move.'

'Max Brigstock may not be quite the dyed-in-the-wool villain I first thought, Mother, but that doesn't mean I like him personally any better. He rubs me up the wrong way somehow.' Jane grimaced. 'Mind you, at the moment it doesn't take much!'

The day was trying. The telephone rang constantly with what seemed like a phone call from every friend Jane had, full of curiosity or commiseration, according to persona. Having braced herself each time the phone rang in case one of the callers should be Adrian, by the middle of the afternoon Jane was a mass of jangling nerves.

'Tomorrow,' she said passionately, 'I vote we go out— away from that wretched telephone. I hate Alexander Graham Bell!'

'If he hadn't invented it someone else would have,' observed her mother. 'Why not go out now? Go for a stroll by the river, or something. Weather like this isn't so common that one should waste it indoors.'

Jane jumped to her feet eagerly. 'Are you sure you don't mind being left with the telephone for company?'

'I shall take it off the hook and have a nap until you get back,' Mrs Calvert promised serenely.

The afternoon was hot and still with surprisingly few people about for such a beautiful day. Jane wandered along the familiar footpath, deep in her own thoughts, oblivious of her surroundings as she mulled over the problematical turn her life had taken; until she realised with annoyance that her feet had brought her to the place she had always run to for privacy, except that these days it was somewhere she had no right to be. Her secret retreat as a child had always been this little inlet in the river where tree-roots formed shallow steps right down to the water. Unfortunately it now belonged to Max Brigstock, and the sensible thing to do would be to get out of there as quickly as she could. But the shade of the overhanging willows was so inviting that Jane decided to take the gamble and risk a moment or two's rest before retracing her footsteps.

She kicked off her shoes and stretched out on the grass, her eyelids heavy as she watched dragonflies skim over the sunlit surface of the water... and the next thing she knew she was waking up with a start from a heavy doze, shivering because a tall shadow was blocking off the sun's warmth.

'You're trespassing again, Miss Calvert,' observed Max Brigstock pleasantly, and Jane scrambled to her feet, her face hot with embarrassment as she searched for her shoes.

'I apologise—again,' she said tightly, brushing down the skirt of her green cotton dress. 'I was—rather abstracted, I'm afraid, and found I'd wandered here without knowing it.'

'Force of habit, no doubt.' He reached out a hand to detach a twig from her tousled hair.

Jane stepped back a little, mortified to find herself flustered by his touch. 'Since I'm trespassing I'd better take myself off.'

Max Brigstock gave her a very unexpected smile. 'I won't prosecute, I promise.'

Jane shook her hair back from her face, eyeing him uncertainly. 'I used to come here a lot when I was young, you see—it was my secret hideaway.'

'And now I've intruded and spoilt it for you!'

'Hardly! I mean, it *is* your property.'

'I imagine it's difficult for you to get used to that, if you've always had the run of the place.' Max Brigstock leaned comfortably against the trunk of an oak tree. 'I rarely have the time to walk here myself, so please feel free to wander here at will. *I* won't mind.'

Jane felt as if the ground were shifting beneath her feet like quicksand. 'How—how kind.'

He laughed. 'Don't sound so amazed. I *can* be kind, you know.'

'Yes, of course.' Jane edged away a little. 'I'd better be going.'

'Don't run away just because I'm here.' He slid gracefully, until he was sitting on the grass with his back to the trunk of the tree. He patted the ground beside him. 'Won't you join me and let me apologise for the terrible gaffe I made last night?'

Jane was so surprised, she did as he said, subsiding on the grass with her hands clasped about her knees as she shot him a rather conciliatory look. 'No apology necessary, I assure you. You weren't to know I'd called off my wedding, after all.'

Max looked at her in silence for a moment. He was dressed casually in well-worn sailcloth trousers, with a cotton polo shirt not unlike the colour of his eyes, she noted absently, and his hair was damp as though he'd just been for a swim.

'Would you jump up and run away in high dudgeon if I asked you *why* you called it off?' he said eventually.

Jane shook her head. 'No.' She bowed her head, studying her clasped hands. 'It wasn't something I did lightly, believe me. I hated having to hurt Adrian.'

'Are you saying you suffered a change of heart?' he prompted quietly.

Jane looked up to meet green-flecked hazel eyes utterly lacking in the mockery she'd been expecting. 'It was my mind I changed rather than my heart,' she said ruefully. 'I don't *think* I'm basically fickle. It was more a case of realising before it was too late that my heart had never really been involved. I would have liked it to be, but it wasn't. Which didn't seem to be a very good basis for a successful marriage.' She flushed suddenly under his intent scrutiny. 'I really don't know why I'm telling you all this.'

'Perhaps because I asked,' he said softly.

Jane eyed him curiously. 'And do people always do what you ask?'

'Always.' Max rose to his feet in one powerful movement and bent to hold out his hand to her. 'Though, to be honest,' he added, as he pulled her to her feet, 'I think I should make it clear that I'm more accustomed to giving orders than requests.'

Jane removed her hand hurriedly, before he could guess at her reaction to his touch. What on earth was the matter with her? she thought irritably. She must be run down, or something. Then she realised that she was wasting a golden opportunity, and turned the full wattage of her warmest smile on her companion.

'Mr Brigstock——'

'Won't you call me Max?'

Jane nodded. 'Very well. Max, then. I was about to say that, because I've got this unexpected opportunity, I wonder if I could revert to yesterday——'

'Which particular part of yesterday do you have in mind?' he interrupted drily. 'It was a fairly eventful day, from my point of view.'

Jane laughed, feeling suddenly confident in Max Brigstock's company for the first time. 'You mean you don't have vengeful females descending on you out of the blue very often!'

'None like you, certainly,' he assured her and smiled, his eyes gleaming in a very unsettling manner.

Jane's pulse accelerated. Was he actually flirting with her? Her smile deepened. 'Mr—Max, I mean. Now that we know each other slightly better, isn't it possible that we could come to some sort of agreement over Dower Cottage? I hate the thought of having to leave it. I was born there. It's always been my home. Couldn't you let us stay? Please?'

The warmth drained from Max Brigstock's face. He stepped back, only a few inches or so, but enough to make it clear that he was distancing himself from Jane with intent.

'No chance, Miss Calvert,' he said brusquely. 'Not even when you ask so very beguilingly. I'm sure no one has ever refused when you said "please" in your entire life, but I'm afraid I must be the exception. Dower Cottage belongs to me, and I need it. I'm afraid the soft words and the smiles were wasted.'

Jane stood very still for a moment. His refusal was a bitter blow, both to her hopes and to something else she decided must be her vanity. Somehow she not only achieved a smile, but a philosophical shrug to go with it. 'Oh, well, it was a good try.'

'Very good!' he agreed, the mockery back in full force in his eyes. 'For a moment there I was sorely tempted to give in and say yes, even though I pride myself on my lack of susceptibility where feminine wiles are concerned.'

'Do you, indeed?' Jane looked at her watch. 'Well, since there's no point at all in wasting my time here any further, I'll be off. Mother must be wondering where I am.'

'I'll walk back with you to the edge of the wood.' He fell in step beside Jane as she moved away.

'There's no need, thank you just the same,' she said shortly, eager to rid herself of his company now that she'd made a fool of herself about Dower Cottage yet again. 'Nothing untoward's likely to happen to me in broad daylight on a Sunday afternoon.'

'I'm sure you're right,' he countered, sounding bored. 'Just the same I'd prefer to return you safely to Dower Cottage.'

Jane shot him a fulminating glance. 'Make sure the trespasser's off your property, you mean.'

'Not at all.' He smiled gently. 'Dower Cottage *is* my property!'

The rest of the walk was made in such uncomfortable silence that Jane almost broke into a run as they reached the familiar paddock.

'Right,' she said curtly. 'Mission accomplished—Mr Brigstock.'

He took her hand to help her over the stile, retaining his grasp even after Jane was on the ground on the other side. 'Peace of mind,' he said pensively, 'isn't something I associate with you, Miss Jane Calvert. In our brief but eventful acquaintance so far, the atmosphere tends more to the war-like, wouldn't you say?' He released her hand, smiling at her. 'Until tomorrow, then.'

'Goodbye, Mr Brigstock.'

'I thought I was Max,' he reminded her.

'I think I'd prefer it if we kept to the formalities,' she returned with hauteur.

'By all means. Goodbye then—Miss Calvert.' With a mock salute Max turned and strolled away in a leisurely fashion which made Jane grit her teeth as she turned on her heel to hurry towards the house.

The encounter did nothing to improve Jane's general mood, particularly when her mother learned that her daughter had taken it into her head to plead yet again to stay at the cottage. Mrs Calvert told Jane in no uncertain terms that her behaviour was quite irrational, and in future to leave the subject of Dower Cottage entirely alone.

'*You* may be set on keeping it, Jane, but I am not. Somewhere more convenient and in better repair would suit me very nicely, so please try to be a little more civilised when Mr Brigstock calls round tomorrow evening. Try not to bristle so much in his vicinity—anyone would think you resent the fact that he's attractive as much as you resent his taking on the role of village squire.'

'I do not!' said Jane indignantly. 'Besides, I don't think he *is* all that attractive.'

'Liar! Anyway,' said Olivia Calvert with a sigh, 'I'm going to bed. I'm dog-tired.'

Jane felt a sharp stab of compunction at the weariness on her mother's face. 'Mother, I'm sorry. All this hassle is wearing you out, and it's all my fault.'

'I'll survive, child,' Mrs Calvert bent to kiss her daughter goodnight. 'Now don't stay up too late. A good night's sleep wouldn't do you any harm, either, I fancy.'

Jane turned on the television when she was alone, switching channels until a programme about varying types of architecture caught her fancy. Its theme was the familiar one of the tussle between old and classical and new and innovative, and she watched idly for a while, until the name Brigstock, along with a shot of a tenement block in the East End of London, brought her bolt upright on the sofa. The split-screen shot showed both how the Edwardian building had looked a few years before and how it looked now, after its extensive refurbishment. This, the presenter informed Jane, had been carried out only after full consultation with the existing tenants, and provided a variety of improvements, including a number of sheltered homes within the development complete with warden. The entire project had been made possible, Jane learned, startled, by the philanthropic interest and support of one of a new breed of property developers, Max Brigstock, who, as the woman said archly, seemed certain to be *Sir* Max one day. He was currently engaged in a new project near his home, where a slum area by the name of Pipers Flats was to be converted into low-rent, attractive housing within reach of the average working-man's pocket.

'Mother!' yelled Jane, racing upstairs. 'You'll never guess what I've just heard.'

Olivia Calvert sat bolt upright in bed, her hand clapped to her chest dramatically. 'Lord knows. Break it to me gently!'

Jane spent the following morning ringing up friends to ask them to keep an ear open for any jobs on offer, then turned her attention to the garden, deciding that some hard physical labour was probably the best remedy for her present state of unrest. By five that evening she was sweating and filthy and nothing in the world seemed more important than a long, leisurely bath.

'Don't forget Mr Brigstock's coming round,' her mother reminded her as her daughter made a bee-line for the bathroom.

'As if I could! Anyway, he's coming to see you, not me, Mother dear,' said Jane tartly.

'Nevertheless, I'd still like you to be on hand, preferably with a smile on your face if you can manage it. Your expression yesterday was enough to turn the milk sour.'

Jane giggled. 'I'll be good, I promise. Only just let me get a few layers of dust and good honest sweat off first!'

Jane felt considerably better when she went downstairs later, cool in a white-dotted yellow cotton dress, every gleaming hair in place, with even a touch of lipstick and mascara added as a gesture of appeasement to her mother.

'Darling, you do look nice,' said her mother, beaming. 'Have a drink; you deserve one after all that digging.'

Jane accepted a generous gin and tonic gratefully, then curled up on the window-seat to enjoy it in the breeze filtering through the open window while Mrs Calvert watched a television newscast. Jane gazed out over the flower-beds she'd weeded so energetically, feeling rather pleased with herself after her labours. Then the telephone rang. She groaned histrionically but her mother held up a hand, smiling in triumph.

'Let it ring, love. Ben fixed the answerphone while you were in the bath. I want to see if it works.'

'Brilliant!'

After the telephone stopped ringing Jane waited, then pressed the button to find out who'd called. 'Perhaps it's Max Brigstock,' she said hopefully, 'saying he can't make it tonight.'

It was not Max Brigstock. After the tone there was a silence so lengthy that Jane thought no message had been recorded, then Adrian's furious voice said, 'Jane! I must speak to you. This can't...'

But he'd left it too long. Whatever else he'd wanted to say was cut off.

'Oh, dear!' said Mrs Calvert. 'Adrian sounds in a bit of a state.'

Jane blew out her cheeks. 'He certainly does. I'd begun to hope he might go off to the States without any more argument, but I suppose that was unrealistic. He does so detest answering machines, too,' she added with a grin.

'Which, no doubt, is why you were so eager to have yours installed here,' said her mother drily.

'Well—yes, partly. But I promise *you'll* find it handy, too.'

'That's what Ben said, when he put the extra power-point in for me. He watched that programme last night with Daisy, by the way.'

'What programme?'

'Oh, really, Jane, don't be tiresome. The one where Max Brigstock was mentioned, of course. They were most impressed. Particularly by the bit about Pipers Flats.'

'Local boy makes good—too good to be true, in my opinion.'

'Since the man's due here any minute I'd prefer it if you kept it to yourself. Now do be civil!'

Jane smiled demurely. 'I'll be good—promise.'

She was back at her post at the window-seat, knees drawn up to her chin, when the expected figure turned in through the gate. Max Brigstock had obviously decided to combine his evening fitness session with the visit to Dower Cottage.

Jane uncurled herself from her perch and went to let him in.

'Good evening, Mr Brigstock.' She smiled up at him with a *bonhomie* imparted by her gin and tonic, so obviously startling him that her smile widened naughtily.

'Good evening. I'm sorry I'm late,' he said, eying her warily. 'I walked down and rather misjudged the time.'

'No problem. What would you like to drink?' asked Jane, deliberately gracious as she ushered him into the sitting-room.

'I don't suppose you'd have a beer?'

Olivia Calvert smiled as she rose to welcome him. 'Good evening, Mr Brigstock. Come and sit down. And we do have some beer, Jane. I keep it for the lad who helps in the garden.'

Jane went off to fetch it, humming to herself as she rummaged for an old glass tankard of her father's. She pulled a face as it rattled a little against the cans of bitter she had arranged on the tray. Perhaps it might have been wiser to eat something before embarking on the gin and tonic which, for once, she had felt in need of quite badly. Probably because the boy wonder was coming! Not that he looked much of a danger at the moment, she decided, as she returned to the others. Dark head bent towards her mother, immaculate in designer suit and ice-blue shirt, he looked as if butter wouldn't melt in his mouth.

Max Brigstock accepted the beer gratefully, then unfastened his briefcase.

'Take your time, Mr Brigstock,' said Olivia, as Jane returned to her post at the window. 'Relax, enjoy your beer for a bit before we plunge into business matters.'

Her guest smiled at her. Despite his immaculate appearance he looked weary, with dark smudges of fatigue below the bright, light eyes.

'I've had a hectic day,' he admitted, then leaned forward slightly. 'Mrs Calvert, I'd be very pleased if you'd call me Max.'

'*Sir* Max one day, according to the television,' said Jane from the window.

'Typical media exaggeration,' he said quietly.

Mrs Calvert speared Jane with a look, then smiled warmly at her guest. 'I'd be delighted to call you Max. I'm a little on the elderly side for you to be happy with my first name, I imagine, but please don't be formal with my daughter. As you know, she's plain Jane.'

'Scarcely an apt description,' he said, as if he knew it was expected of him, and took some brochures from the briefcase.

Jane slid gracefully off the window-seat and strolled across to the sofa, looking over her mother's shoulder at the house descriptions he produced.

'Perhaps you'd like to give an opinion on which would suit your mother best,' he suggested.

Jane shrugged. 'My opinion wouldn't count for much. It's impossible for me to think of anywhere but Dower Cottage as home.'

Max Brigstock looked at her levelly. 'But I thought it was a case of which one suited your mother best, Miss—Jane.' He turned to Olivia, who was looking on with enjoyment. 'This one, Pond House, is slightly larger than Dower Cottage, but needs a fair amount of redecoration. The Ducklings, on the other hand—the small Georgian house at the end of Friary Lane—is in excellent condition, but the garden's on the large side.'

'My mother's always been used to a large garden!' said Jane at once.

Mrs Calvert touched her daughter's hand. 'True, but I'm not getting any younger, darling. Actually, I'd be very happy with that little back garden at Pond House, which is a place I've always liked, you know. I used to visit old Miss Braithwaite there a lot during her last illness.'

Jane felt utterly deflated. She realised, with shame, that it was high time she began to think of what her mother really wanted, rather than rushing in with her own ideas on the subject. And to make matters worse she suspected that Max Brigstock was reading her mind, and was in total agreement.

'Fetch Max another beer please, Jane,' said Mrs Calvert, and Jane went off with alacrity, glad of a moment on her own to regroup her forces. She decided to allow herself a second, much smaller drink, just to keep her spirits up until Max took his leave but, to her dismay, when she joined the others she found that her mother had invited Max to share their supper.

'That's if you don't mind cold chicken and potato salad and so on in the kitchen,' said Olivia cheerfully.

Max smiled at her with a warmth which clearly charmed Olivia, its effect on Jane something she preferred not to analyse.

'I can think of nothing I'd like better, Mrs Calvert,' he said, with such sincerity that Olivia beamed and jumped to her feet.

'Splendid. You stay here and talk to Jane while I throw it together. Most of it's ready, anyway. Shan't be long.'

Max eyed Jane quizzically when they were alone. 'You would have preferred me to refuse, I think.'

Jane shrugged, curling up in an armchair with her drink. 'Not at all. Mother's a hospitable soul. I'm used to unexpected guests at mealtimes.' She remembered her mother's instructions to be pleasant, and gave him a smile which brought a questioning look to Max Brigstock's eyes as they rested on her graceful, lounging figure.

'If the situation had been different,' he began, surprising her, 'with no Dower Cottage standing between us like the Berlin wall, would you have been any more warmly disposed towards me, do you think, Jane? As a mere acquaintance, of course!'

Jane thought it over. 'I don't really know. Even without the wicked landlord bit, we got off to a bad start anyway, didn't we, when I knocked you off your bicycle!'

He grinned, and sat forward, setting his tankard down on the low table in front of him. 'It lacked finesse as an introduction, certainly.'

Jane smiled back rather uncertainly. 'I've been a bit of a nuisance really, haven't I?'

'Understandable. Loss of job, home and bridegroom all in the space of days must have been a bit of a tough mouthful to swallow and still keep smiling.'

Jane looked at him searchingly, but there was no mockery in the light, intent eyes. Max Brigstock's face wore a look of friendly sympathy, in fact, and she responded to it quite naturally, smiling at him with a warmth which he plainly found beguiling.

'Poor chap,' he said, shaking his head. 'The man you found you couldn't marry,' he explained in answer to her questioning look. 'He can't be very happy at this moment.'

'No,' agreed Jane soberly. 'I don't think he is. Poor Adrian.'

'Poor Adrian indeed.'

Olivia Calvert's reappearance came almost as an intrusion into the unexpected moment of rapport, and it was with a feeling verging on regret that Jane went with the others to share the second meal in as many days with the new owner of Verney House.

The occasion was no ordeal either, Jane found, as Max Brigstock talked with far less constraint at her mother's table than at the Whiteheads' the previous Saturday. The conversation over the meal was lively, and by the coffee stage Jane had begun to wonder why she'd ever been so defensive towards Max Brigstock in the first place. She actually liked him, she realised with a start, as she watched him laughing with her mother over some village anecdote that Olivia was recounting in her usual astringent style. Max looked across at Jane, grinning, to see if she was sharing the joke—then frowned, arrested, as he found Jane regarding him with an expression that he'd never seen before. His eyes, glittering with unspoken question, locked with her wondering, tawny gaze until Jane's lashes fell, colour rising in her cheeks, and Mrs Calvert returned things to normal by suggesting coffee and brandy in the sitting-room. Max accepted with an eagerness which suggested that evenings of such simple domesticity were a rare event for him, and it was with obvious reluctance that he returned later to the reason for his visit. He addressed himself very directly to Olivia Calvert, avoiding Jane's eyes.

'Before I forget, Mrs Calvert,' he said, 'I should like to make it clear at this point that I will bear all costs of redecoration, or repairs, for your new home since you will be, in effect, my tenant.'

Jane's eyes widened. 'I don't understand. Do you mean that you're purchasing this house solely for my mother to live in it?'

He looked across at her, nodding in agreement. 'Exactly. Mrs Calvert will enjoy life tenancy at whichever house she chooses.' His eyes lit with a sudden, unholy gleam. 'I am, after all, turning your mother out of hearth and home, according to you, am I not? Think of the damage to my philanthropic image if I failed to provide her with somewhere else to live!'

Only a few hours earlier Jane would have risen to the bait but now, after discovering that she could like Max Brigstock quite a lot, given half a chance, she smiled back at him, much to her mother's satisfaction.

'I admit that I misread the situation first off,' she said ruefully, 'but my mother soon put me right about the facts.' She caught her mother's eye, then went on with purpose. 'I'd like to apologise sincerely for my interference. I've acted all along on impulse, without going into the situation fully enough.'

'Jane has been under some stress lately,' put in Mrs Calvert.

'I'm sure Max doesn't want to hear any more about that,' said Jane quickly, colouring.

Max smiled at her, in a warmer, softer way that she found very much to her taste. 'Thank you for the apology, Jane. I accept unreservedly, and suggest that we put previous differences in the past, where they belong. I'm sorry I had to be the one cast for the role of wicked landlord, but I promise, Mrs Calvert, that you won't lose by it. Just let me know which house you finally decide on and I'll see to the rest.'

It was raining heavily with the sudden force of a summer shower when their guest was ready to go. Mrs Calvert insisted on lending Max an old golf umbrella for the walk home, and as the three of them gathered in the doorway no one noticed the man advancing militantly up the path, mainly because Max and Jane were huddled together under the decrepit old umbrella, laughing as she alerted him to the worst of the holes in it, his head bent towards hers in unconscious intimacy.

'Jane!' thundered Dr Adrian Fry, in a voice which shook with suppressed passion.

'Why, Adrian,' said Mrs Calvert, with remarkable aplomb. 'What a surprise!'

Max Brigstock's sharp eyes flew from the sudden dismay on Jane's face to the furious affront on that of the slim, fair stranger, whose identity was obvious from the first.

Jane's heart took a nose-dive, but she smiled valiantly. 'Hello, Adrian. Let me introduce you. Dr Adrian Fry, Mr Max Brigstock.'

'Max is our next-door neighbour,' Mrs Calvert informed him.

'Dr Fry,' said Max, with a brief incline of his head, and held out a hand which Adrian ignored rudely, his face suffused with angry colour.

'So that's it—*now* I know the truth!' he blurted, glaring at Jane, who frowned at him in surprise. Adrian's manners were normally impeccable.

'Adrian——' she began, but he ignored her, shaking a fist in Max's startled face.

'You're the reason she threw me over like this, I suppose,' he said hoarsely. 'I might have known there was another man in it. All that nonsense about saving me unhappiness in the future...'

'I think you're labouring under a misapprehension,' drawled Max, beginning to look dangerous.

'Max had nothing to *do* with it, Adrian,' interrupted Jane hastily. 'You're barking up the wrong tree.' She turned to Max in desperation. 'Thank you so much for bringing the information from the estate agent.' Her eyes met his beseechingly, and Max responded to it instantly, covering his anger with a smile of glittering reassurance.

'Not at all, Jane. My pleasure.' He turned to Mrs Calvert, who was looking on with rather ill-concealed enjoyment. 'Goodnight, Mrs Calvert, thank you for dinner. Once again, it's been a very enjoyable evening.'

This was too much for Adrian, who looked ready to explode, and Jane grabbed Max by the hand, literally dragging him down the path towards the gate out of earshot.

'I'm going, I'm going,' he said, shaking with laughter. 'But I'm more than willing to stay and take up the cudgels for you.'

'No fear,' said Jane fervently, glancing back towards the house, where her mother was obviously having difficulty in restraining Adrian from coming after them. 'I'm terribly sorry about all that——'

'Don't be. I quite enjoyed the role thrust on me by your ex-fiancé,' Max assured her, grinning from ear to ear under the umbrella, which was doing very little to keep them both dry. He sobered abruptly. 'Tell me the truth, Jane. Any regrets? *Do* you want to marry the man, after all?'

'No,' she said without hesitation.

Max's eyes gleamed as he shot a look in Adrian's direction. 'Then I think your Dr Fry needs convincing of the fact, don't you?' And before Jane could guess what he had in mind, Max swept her into his arms under the umbrella and kissed her with such possessive thoroughness that she was speechless with surprise, and several other emotions, by the time he released her. 'Goodnight,' he said, and smiled into her stunned face before strolling away through the rain, leaving Jane to trail back up the path with a sinking heart.

'Why couldn't you have told me the truth?' Adrian said scornfully. 'What possible competition could I be with the filthy-rich boy "next door"—as you so humorously describe his luxury mansion, Mrs Calvert.'

'Don't you vent your spleen on my mother!' flared Jane. 'If you're spoiling for a fight, keep to the right opponent.'

'Added to which,' added Mrs Calvert with dignity, 'I suggest that you come inside and do whatever fighting you have in mind, verbal or otherwise, in the privacy of my home.'

The slight emphasis on the last two words brought a flush to Adrian's lean cheeks. 'I'm sorry, Mrs Calvert,' he said stiffly. 'I have no argument with you, of course.'

'No, you don't,' she agreed, leading the way into the sitting-room. 'But I can understand that you feel Jane has a lot to answer for. Nevertheless, please remember that she is my daughter, and that you are under *my* roof, Adrian. I shall go upstairs and turn up my portable television very loudly, while you have your say. Jane,' she added, with a look at her daughter, 'please offer Adrian a drink.'

'Adrian doesn't drink,' Jane reminded her, and smiled with a hectic brilliance that Mrs Calvert noted with misgiving. 'Thank you for your forbearance, Mother. We shan't keep you locked in durance vile for long.'

'I'm glad you think the occasion calls for levity,' said Adrian bitterly once they were alone.

'If I sounded flippant I'm sorry,' said Jane, and waved her former fiancé to a chair, steeling herself for the inevitable.

However much Jane kept telling herself that she deserved it, the following half-hour was a deeply unpleasant experience. Adrian Fry was determined to let Jane know how incensed he was by her behaviour, and went on at great length about the appalling treatment he'd undergone at her hands, and the fact that she had been dishonest about her reasons and had never mentioned Max Brigstock when she called the wedding off. Jane sat, mute, letting his tide of hurt and anger and resentment flow over her unchecked, until he wound up with a magnanimous offer to forget all her foolishness if she would just come to her senses and go on with the ceremony as planned at the end of the week.

'Why?' asked Jane baldly.

Adrian stared at her, thunderstruck. 'What do you mean, "why"?'

'Why do you want me to go on with the wedding?'

'Really, Jane, don't be childish!'

But Jane persisted, determined to make Adrian list his reasons one by one, listening patiently while he used words like inconvenience and irresponsibility, and talked of arrangements and plans upset by her irrational behaviour. Jane heard him out in silence wondering, as she looked at Adrian objectively, why she had ever seriously contemplated marriage with this logical, clever man, who used disruption of arrangements as his strongest argument to persuade her to reconsider her decision.

'You've never mentioned love,' she pointed out wistfully, and Adrian flushed, as though she'd said something improper.

'That, of course, goes without saying,' he said, his eyes sliding away from the wide, tawny gaze fixed on him.

'But it shouldn't,' said Jane gently. 'A girl needs to be told she's loved and wanted, Adrian.'

'Are you sure you don't mean sex!' Adrian sneered, and jumped to his feet angrily, accusing her of using sentiment and emotion to fog up the issue. Whereupon Jane interrupted him by declaring that since these qualities were inherent in her nature he should be grateful to be well shot of her; and suddenly Adrian turned on her with a malevolence which shook her to the core.

'Why not be honest, Jane,' he snarled, 'and admit that the real reason for your U-turn was the man I met on your doorstep tonight. Max Brigstock, from where I was standing, seemed more than suitable for your sexual requirements.' He gave a disgusted snort. 'Power and money are the ultimate aphrodisiacs, I read somewhere, so how can a poor scientist like me hope to compete with a jumped-up barrow-boy of a millionaire like Max Brigstock!'

At which Jane lost her temper completely, and expelled her former fiancé from the premises, almost chasing him to the car parked in the lane outside, not satisfied until she'd seen him disappear into the distance in a cloud of exhaust-fumes, as he gunned his car down the road with a disregard for his gearbox normally foreign to the disciplined Dr Adrian Fry.

'I know that I deserved most of what he said,' declared Jane tearfully, over a hot drink later with her mother. 'And I'm well aware that Adrian is entitled to feel the way he does. But when he accused me of ditching him for Max Brigstock's money I saw red.'

'It was unfortunate that Adrian chose that particular moment to put in an appearance,' said Mrs Calvert pensively. 'After all, Max is a very—very eye-catching sort of man. It's only natural that Adrian thought the worst. Particularly since Max took it into his head to kiss you goodnight, Jane.'

Jane flushed. 'He acted on impulse, that's all. Said something about convincing Adrian about my decision.' She leaned her chin on her hands. 'On the other hand maybe it was a good thing. Adrian probably finds it easier to believe that I deserted him for another man rather than the real reason.'

'More than likely, love.'

Jane sniffed hard, and gave herself a little shake. 'Anyway, let's forget Adrian and talk about something much more important.' She eyed her mother challengingly. 'Tell me the truth—no prevaricating, now. Are you really, really happy about moving to Pond House?'

'Yes. Very. This place is getting to be a burden, especially the garden. Three acres is a lot for a woman on her own. And you were the one who reminded me I wasn't getting any younger, remember.'

Jane's reddened eyes filled with remorse. 'Lord, I'm sorry, Mother. I've been thoughtless, haven't I? And I don't know why I'm making such a fuss. Wherever you choose to live will always be home, anyway, as far as I'm concerned.'

'Except when you have a home of your own, Jane.'

Jane smiled ruefully. 'Which won't be yet awhile, now, will it? No—don't get up—I'll make some more chocolate. You sit down and rest.'

'Decrepitude isn't a sudden affliction, Jane. It's a gradual process!'

'I know, I know. Nevertheless, I think it's high time I stopped taking you for granted.'

Secretly Jane was mortified that she'd been so taken up with her own dismay at leaving Dower Cottage that she'd never given a thought to her mother's feelings. In bed that night she lay awake for a long time, shaken and restless, not only by the visit from Adrian on top of the evening with Max, but by her own blindness to the burden the house had become to her mother. The thatch was due to be renewed, the central heating system was on its last legs and a lot of redecoration was needed, to name only a few items Mrs Calvert had been worrying about for some time. Jane knew that it was useless to bring her father into it. George Calvert had never wanted to live in Dower Cottage from the first, and had always resented the fact that only his wife's Verney connections made the tenancy possible.

But as sleep finally overtook her it was not her mother, nor the cottage, nor even Adrian, who monopolised Jane's last waking thoughts. It was the memory of Max Brigstock's mouth, warm and hard, with an undisguised demand in his kiss which had sent trickles cascading down her spine quite unrelated to the rain spattering on them through the holes of the ridiculous old umbrella.

CHAPTER FOUR

LIFE was less exacting over the next few days. The weather was dry and hot, Adrian was heard from no more, and once the ill-fated wedding-day had passed without incident Jane began to relax a little. Mrs Calvert had duly settled on Pond House, the rent for which, Max Brigstock made clear in writing, would be the same as she paid for Dower Cottage.

'I still can't make out why he's doing this,' said Jane suspiciously. 'It doesn't seem feasible, somehow.'

'Perhaps he looks on me as his entrée into Wyndcombe society,' said her mother with a grin, which faded quickly as Jane scowled. 'Joke, darling! Whatever's happened to your sense of humour these days?'

Jane apologised, well aware that she was difficult to live with at the moment. Her most pressing problem was that, whereas a short time ago she'd had a busy, fulfilling job and a home of her own, not to mention a prospective husband, now all three were a thing of the past and she was at such a loose end it was driving her crazy. With grim determination she threw herself into the constant task of keeping the garden under control, and weeded and mowed and clipped with an application which did wonders for channelling her body's energy, but nothing at all for her mind, which was left fancy-free to mull endlessly over the problem of her future.

Then one evening Mrs Calvert went off to play bridge at the Whiteheads', and for a time after she'd gone Jane tried to lose herself in the book she was reading. Admitting defeat at last, she decided that the evening was so lovely that a walk might burn off some of the excess energy she'd accumulated, and help with her ridiculous secret disappointment because Max Brigstock had made no move to contact her personally after Adrian's visit. Obviously he'd been amusing himself, she decided. No doubt he thought the whole thing was a big joke.

Jane locked up the house and set off briskly, deciding to do the thing properly by taking the footpath which led on a five-mile circuit around Wyndcombe. After an hour of rapid walking she took a rest by the river bank under a fringe of willows, pitching pebbles idly into the current, but when the light started to fade she began to make her way back, her pace less energetic as she made for home. Then suddenly the quiet evening was shattered by the wail of sirens in the distance, and she frowned, breaking into a run, her heart suddenly thumping with cold premonition. Jane ran like the wind, her worst fears confirmed as she came in sight of Dower Cottage, where two fire-engines were directing their hoses on the blazing thatch directly above her own room. She could see the Whiteheads struggling to restrain her mother from getting too close to the house. As Jane thrust her way frantically through a knot of local people, a smoke-blackened figure shot out through the front door.

'She's not there, Mrs Calvert,' it croaked, and before Jane could reach her Olivia Calvert dropped to the grass in a dead faint.

'Mother!' screamed Jane, and threw herself forward, jostling Daisy and Ben Whitehead out of the way as she dropped to her knees beside her mother, almost beside herself with panic.

'Give her some air, for goodness' sake,' said the voice of authority, as the smoke-smeared man, who proved to be Max Brigstock, Jane saw with dull surprise, tersely ordered the crowd to give way.

Jane heard someone sobbing loudly, then forgot everything as Olivia's eyelids fluttered open and she looked straight up into Jane's streaming eyes.

'Do stop—making such—a noise, darling,' said Olivia faintly. 'I'm quite—all right.'

'Oh, Mother, Mother,' said Jane brokenly, aware now that it was her own sobs she could hear. 'You frightened me to death.'

'*You* frightened *her*!' said a furious voice and Jane looked up, startled, into Max Brigstock's filthy face. 'Why do you think your mother collapsed, you stupid girl? She thought you were *in* there, up in your room!'

'But I—I just went for a walk,' faltered Jane, too shocked even to feel angry at his manner. Her knees trembled as she hurried after Ben Whitehead, who was carrying her mother to the car. 'I was hot, Mother, so I went down the path to the river.'

'There, there, Jane,' said Ben soothingly, as he helped Olivia gently into his car. 'Your mother will be fine in a minute or two.'

'I'm perfectly all right,' said Olivia in a stronger voice. She smiled up at Jane. 'Now I know *you* are! Could you bear to hang on and see how much actual damage has been done before you join us, darling? I can't think how it happened. Neither of us smokes.'

'Don't worry about that now, Liv,' said Daisy Whitehead firmly, and got in the back seat to put an arm about her friend.

'I'll stay here with your daughter, Mrs Calvert,' added Max Brigstock, and received a smile of gratitude before the car moved off.

Jane turned back to the chaotic scene in despair. The fire was out by this time, but a gaping hole in the thatch was still giving off black smoke and two of the firemen were keeping their hoses directed at it. While people from the village offered sympathy to Jane, Max Brigstock organised some willing male helpers into a tidying-up operation to get broken glass out of the way. He returned to instruct Jane to keep well clear for the moment.

'I'll go inside now with a couple of the firemen and check the house out thoroughly,' he said, in a voice hoarse from smoke.

'Can't I go with you?' she pleaded.

'No! Keep out of the way, please.'

Jane was recovered enough to feel resentment at his high-handed manner by this time, and stood fuming in frustration as he disappeared inside the cottage. She turned as a hand touched her arm, and stared blankly at the young woman smiling ruefully at her.

'I'm Liz Collins, Miss Calvert. We met the other day. My husband Jim and I work for Mr Brigstock.'

Jane smiled in apology. 'Of course—so sorry, Mrs Collins. I'm in a bit of a daze, I'm afraid.'

'Hardly surprising.' The woman waved in the direction of a rustic bench at the end of the lawn. 'Come and sit down over there. I've brought a few flasks of coffee down. Jim can see to the others. You come with me— you're shaking.'

Jane found that she was very glad indeed to sit down, and even more glad of the steaming coffee her companion poured into a paper cup for her. 'That's wonderful. Thank you so much. Lord knows how long it will be before I can get to a kettle.'

'I don't suppose you *will* be able to tonight. Not until they know the extent of the damage.'

Jane stared in dismay. 'But the fire affected only one small part of the thatch.' She shot to her feet as Max Brigstock emerged from the house and came quickly towards them.

'Is the fire out?' she asked quickly.

'Yes. It was confined to one room, fortunately.'

'Which one?'

'The smallest bedroom.'

Jane gave a smothered sound of distress, and Liz Collins patted her hand.

'Yours?'

Jane nodded dismally, then cleared her throat. 'How about the rest of the house?' she asked Max Brigstock, who was gulping down Liz's coffee thirstily.

'Smoke damage and a few beams affected, but otherwise not too bad. We'll get a better picture in the morning when the usual inspection's been carried out.'

Jane rubbed her smarting eyes. 'May I go inside now?'

'Only if I go with you.'

'It isn't necessary——'

'On the contrary,' he said curtly. 'It's vitally necessary.'

Everyone had gone by this time, bar the firemen. As Jane followed Max into the house she gasped at the heavy reek of damp and smoke in the air, finding it hard to breathe. As Max shone a torch to light their way, Jane stared around her in horror at smoke-blackened walls and dripping curtains.

'Can't we put on the light?'

'No. Wiring's not safe.'

The tour of inspection was short and hideously depressing. Jane's room was a blackened shambles, with nothing worth salvaging. The rest of the bedrooms were soiled and damp, but nothing like as bad as her own.

'Fortunately these old doors are solid oak, which saved the day. The door to the small bedroom was closed,' said Max, and shone the torch on the stairs for Jane to go down. 'It could have been a lot worse. The ground floor hasn't suffered much.'

Jane was silent, utterly harrowed by the sight of her beloved home in such a sorry state.

'Are you all right?' asked Max, before they went outside.

'Yes. Thank you.' Jane frowned suddenly. 'How did you happen to be here?'

'I've been in London for a few days. I'd just got back when I saw the smoke from my bathroom window. I realised that it was coming from your roof, rang the fire brigade then drove down here like a bat out of hell with Jim Collins. We checked that no one was at home and made a start on the roof at once with the garden hose, but the firemen were remarkably prompt. Then your mother arrived with the Whiteheads, frantic because she was certain that you were inside the house, so I went in to make sure.'

Jane peered up at him in the gloom. 'That was very noble of you.'

'Instinct, not heroism. Your mother was in distress so I tried to help. End of story.'

'Thank you, anyway.'

'I don't need *your* thanks, Jane Calvert. What I did I did for your mother, not you.'

Jane stood stunned for a moment, hardly able to recognise this grim stranger as the man who'd kissed her and laughed with her a few short evenings before. She was appalled to find how much his attitude hurt. 'I see. I—I must go and thank your Mrs Collins. She's been very kind.'

Max followed her out into the garden, where the firemen were waiting to leave. Jane thanked them all warmly, one of them had a brief word with Max and soon the fire engines were gone and the garden was quiet, looking oddly deserted as Jim and Liz Collins packed away the empty coffee flasks and paper cups into a basket. Jane expressed her appreciation for their help, then turned to Max.

'Goodnight, then. I'm sorry you've been put to so much trouble.'

Max frowned absently at her, then turned to the others. 'You go on up to the house with Liz in the Land Rover, Jim. I'll take Miss Calvert to the Whiteheads in my car.'

There was silence after the other two had gone. Jane pushed her hair back from her forehead wearily.

'Don't bother to drive me such a short distance. I'll be glad of the walk.'

'I'd rather like to see you off the premises, if you don't mind,' he said curtly, and gestured towards the Aston Martin parked in the lane.

Jane glared at him. 'This happens to be my home. I don't appreciate being ordered out of it as if I were trespassing.'

'No. I imagine it's a new experience for you. Nevertheless, however *you* may think of it, Dower Cottage actually belongs to me.' Max Brigstock looked at her grimly, his eyes hard to read in the soft summer half-darkness. 'I may as well be frank. I'm a man of few illusions.'

Jane looked blank. 'What has that to do with me?'

'I can't help thinking that perhaps a lady who passionately resents giving up her home to a low-bred interloper—like me—might just feel strongly enough to set fire to it rather than allow him the pleasure of possessing it.'

For a moment Jane stared at him, speechless, struggling with outrage and more hurt than she would have believed possible by his accusation. Then her temper boiled over and she slapped the saturnine face hard, with every ounce of strength she could muster.

'How dare you?' she said in a low, shaking voice. 'I suppose to someone like you it's impossible to understand how much this place means to me. That was *my* bedroom that's gutted up there. *Mine!* A piece of my life, gone up in smoke. Good grief, man, I'd no more set Dower Cottage alight than—than set fire to myself!'

Suddenly everything was too much. The strain of the past couple of weeks, crowned tonight by the trauma of the fire, put paid to Jane's self-control completely. She slumped down on the garden seat and put her head in her hands, weeping like a lost soul. Max Brigstock stood watching her woodenly, helpless for once in the face of her distress. 'Miss Calvert—Jane,' he said after a while. 'Please——'

One word from him was enough. Jane straightened and pulled herself together, dashing away her tears with her knuckles. But a great sob tore through her as she got to her feet, and Max Brigstock gave a smothered curse and pulled her into his arms, kissing her with such sudden, tender violence that she melted against him in helpless response for a moment as her mouth parted beneath his. Then sanity returned. Jane gave him a great shove and jumped away, glaring at him.

'Don't touch me!' she spat, shaking back her hair.

Max Brigstock stepped back in silence, and for several tense moments they stood staring at each other like boxers in a ring before the main bout.

'I apologise,' he said at last, through clenched teeth.

'For what, exactly?' she snapped.

'Why, for actually daring to make physical contact with Miss Jane Calvert. What else?'

The contempt in his voice flicked Jane on the raw. 'That was nothing. Less than nothing,' she added, scathingly emphatic. 'I'm more concerned with your accusation of arson. I demand an apology for that, Mr Brigstock.'

'Certainly,' he said calmly. 'You shall have your apology, Miss Calvert, the moment the morning's investigation proves that you merit one. Unless, of course, the indications are to the contrary.'

*   *   *

'Darling! Where on earth have you been?' cried Mrs Calvert, when Jane limped into the Whiteheads' kitchen some time later.

'I wanted Ben to come and fetch you,' said Daisy, pushing Jane down into a chair, 'but Liv said that Mr Brigstock would be bringing you home.'

'He did, in a way,' said Jane, looking at her mother anxiously. 'Are you all right, Mother? Really all right, I mean?'

'I called the doctor,' said Ben reassuringly. 'He gave her the once-over and then stayed for coffee and a chat, which is why I couldn't come after you, my girl.'

'And the doctor's verdict?'

'Said I fainted from fright,' said Mrs Calvert placidly. 'Since I've never done it before I imagine he was right. I was sure you were *in* there, Jane—trapped. It was horrible!'

'Don't think of it!' said Daisy, shuddering, then turned her attention to restoratives for the dishevelled girl slumped at the kitchen table.

'How much damage?' asked Mrs Calvert, while Jane sipped coffee doctored with brandy.

Jane gave a quick account of the cottage's condition and tried to put as good a face as possible on the fact that 'Jane's room' was no more, and that, in fact, apart from a couple of sodden suitcases of clothes in Phillida's room, and the handbag which had fortunately been left in the kitchen, the sum of Jane Calvert's possessions amounted to one car and the grubby jeans and sweat-shirt she was wearing—and that was it.

'In short,' she finished glumly, 'the place is a mess, I'm a mess—life's a mess.'

Mrs Calvert cast a significant look at Ben and Daisy, who immediately announced that it was time for bed and left their guests alone together.

'It's not important, you know, Jane,' said Olivia Calvert gently. 'It's only a house. I can't begin to describe my feelings when I thought you were in there——' She shivered. 'Let's say that all I can think of now is that thank goodness it was just the cottage which suffered, and not you.'

'Max Brigstock thinks I did it,' blurted Jane.

Mrs Calvert frowned. 'Did what?'

'Set fire to Dower Cottage on purpose, would you believe—so that he wouldn't be able to have it.' Jane's laugh was bleak. 'Arson, no less.'

'You must have misunderstood him, Jane!' said her mother, appalled.

'No chance. He made himself quite clear. There's to be an inspection in the morning. Until then, as far as he's concerned, I'm guilty until proved otherwise.' Jane shrugged. 'Not that I care two hoots for Max Brigstock's opinion!' But she did, she realised, with shame. All her life she'd basked in the glow of approval and liking from most people, at home and in school, then in her career. It had been a new and demoralising experience to see contempt in someone's eyes as they looked at her, particularly when the eyes in question were male—and, even more significantly, belonged to Max Brigstock.

'I'll have a word with him tomorrow,' began Mrs Calvert hotly, but Jane shook her head.

'Leave it, Mother. It won't be necessary. He'll be proved wrong, anyway. Whatever caused the fire, it wasn't anything I did. Max Brigstock will be forced to eat his words.' The prospect cheered Jane up a little.

'He must surely have said a thing like that in the heat of the moment, Jane. I can't believe that Max meant such a terrible thing.'

'Oh, yes he did!'

'The drive home can't have been pleasant, then.'

'No.' Jane's smile lit up her grimy face. 'If anyone was about they must have wondered what we were playing at, because I wouldn't set foot in his wretched car after the insult he'd thrown at me, and he was equally determined that I shouldn't walk home alone.'

'So what happened?'

'I trudged here on foot, and he followed behind me in the Aston Martin at a snail's pace, headlights blazing!'

'Oh, Jane!' Mrs Calvert bit her lip, chuckling.

Jane got up, yawning, and asked if Daisy would mind if her latest addition to the roster had a bath, since she was utterly filthy and smelled quite horribly of smoke, and couldn't exist another minute without washing the excesses of the evening away. It was only later, while she marinated up to her chin in hot scented water, that Jane allowed herself to think of her recent arrival at the house. Max Brigstock had jumped out of the car just as she had limped the last yard or so, and had barred her way into the drive, derision plain to see on his dirty face.

'There was no need to follow me here,' she'd told him bitterly. 'Or perhaps you're the sort who makes a habit of kerb-crawling.'

'What a silver-tongued charmer you are, to be sure.' His laugh had set her teeth on edge. 'I promised your mother that I'd see you back, so I did. I couldn't have cared less whether you rode or walked, Miss Jane Calvert, I assure you, and now that my mission's accomplished I'll bid you goodnight.'

And Max Brigstock had driven his Aston Martin off into the moonlight, leaving Jane to think too late of all the clever things she should have said.

CHAPTER FIVE

THE Whitehead household was up and stirring early next morning. Jane, who had opened her eyes on the day with gloom, staggered downstairs yawning, attired in a frivolous pink satin dressing-gown lent by her godmother, to find her mother and Daisy eating some of the latter's special muesli while Ben read them titbits of news from the daily paper. Jane returned the morning greetings, lying politely about her night, which had been the next best thing to sleepless.

'How long will they be on this inspection, do you think?' she asked anxiously.

'Couldn't say.' Ben patted her hand comfortingly. 'Don't worry. You'll know the details soon enough.'

The peace of the breakfast table was shattered a moment later as the kitchen door burst open and in strode a giant, bearded man in a checked shirt and paint-spattered corduroy trousers, his great leonine mane of greying sandy hair on end.

'George!' said Olivia Calvert, astounded. 'What in the world are *you* doing here?'

'Father!' exclaimed Jane.

'Good lord,' said Ben Whitehead, jumping up. 'Daisy, get another cup.'

George Calvert stood with arms akimbo, glaring at the assembled company. 'What's all this about a fire?' he thundered. 'Were you hurt, Olivia—Jane, are you all right? I just came past the cottage and there were people crawling all over it. Why the hell didn't anybody let me know last night?'

'It never occurred to me,' said Olivia calmly. 'Sit down and have some coffee, George, and stop shouting.'

'How about breakfast?' offered Daisy nervously, but the new addition to her guest-list shook his head.

'Never touch it, Daisy. Thank you,' he added, as an afterthought. 'What beats me is why it was up to Daisy to ring me up at first light this morning instead of you, Liv.'

Everyone, including her husband, looked in astonishment at Daisy, who went very pink.

'I thought George had a right to know,' she said defiantly.

Ben Whitehead smiled at his wife, shaking his head in affectionate wonder, then gave a brief account of the events of the night before, and after a time George Calvert calmed down. He took Jane's chair at the table, pulling her on his knee to cuddle her as he had done when she was small.

'Mother fainted,' said Jane huskily against her father's shoulder.

'Good grief!' George Calvert stared at his wife in astonishment. 'What the devil did you do that for, Liv?'

Mrs Calvert closed her eyes for an instant. 'I don't know, George,' she said, opening them again. 'You know how difficult I can be at times.'

'She thought that I was trapped inside,' said Jane, and winced as her father's massive arms tightened round her cruelly at the mere thought. 'She only fainted when she found I wasn't.'

'Sorry, Liv.' George Calvert shook his head in remorse. 'Enough to make anybody faint. Are you all right now?'

His wife gave him a wry little smile. 'More or less, George.'

Suddenly a rap on the kitchen door swivelled all heads in the direction of the man standing there in a grimy coverall and rubber boots, a costume which entirely misled Mr Calvert as to his identity.

'What the hell do you mean by barging in here like that?' he roared.

Max Brigstock's face went rigid with affront. 'I apologise for the intrusion, Mrs Whitehead,' he said, ignoring George Calvert. 'I rang the doorbell, but when no one answered——'

'You came through the garden, of course, Max,' said Olivia with a smile of welcome, and the Whiteheads invited him inside.

George Calvert kept a firm hold on Jane as she tried to leap from his lap. 'Are you the chap in charge of the inspection, then?' he demanded, unabashed. 'From the Fire Brigade, are you? Or are you an insurance chappie?'

'George, do be quiet!' commanded his wife. 'This is Max Brigstock the *owner* of Dower Cottage, if you must know. He owns Verney House now, too,' she added with emphasis, '*and* he happens to be the good Samaritan who searched the blazing cottage for Jane.'

'Only a small part of it was blazing, Mrs Calvert,' Max contradicted, thawing slightly, and George Calvert tipped his daughter from his knee and sprang up to shake Max Brigstock's reluctant hand.

'Well done. I'm in your debt, Brigstock,' he boomed, and Max detached himself and stood back.

'Not at all,' he said colourlessly. His eyes lingered for a moment on Jane, who was busy securing the slippery wrapper around herself, then turned to George Calvert, who was several years younger than his wife and looked several years younger than that.

'Ah, Max,' said Olivia Calvert, her eyes dancing. 'Allow me to present my husband, George Calvert. Jane's father,' she added rather unnecessarily.

Max Brigstock nodded briefly, looking quite obviously sorry that he'd ever set foot across the Whitehead doorstep as he reported that the fire had been caused by faulty wiring. The video recorder in Jane's room was believed to be the culprit.

'Oh, no—I only brought it home with me when—when I came back this time,' said Jane, stricken. 'I'm so sorry, Mother.'

'It wasn't your fault, darling! Any of it,' added Mrs Calvert, with a wry smile at Max.

'The entire cottage needed rewiring years ago,' said Mr Calvert forcefully. 'You wouldn't listen when I told you to pack up and leave the place, Olivia.' His eyes narrowed. 'So what happens now, Brigstock?'

'The cottage will be uninhabitable for some time, I'm afraid, but I'm told that most of the furniture can be salvaged.' Max shot a look at Jane. 'Except for the contents of *your* room, Miss Calvert.'

'I was aware of that last night,' she answered, then looked him very straight in the eye. 'There's no possibility that it was arson, then?' A warm tide of satisfaction rose inside her as Max's jaw clenched visibly.

'Arson?' barked George Calvert.

'I had my suspicions on the subject last night,' admitted Max coolly. 'They were proved wrong, fortunately. I wonder,' he added, 'if I might have a word with Miss Calvert in private?'

'Not until she's got some decent clothes on!' retorted her father.

'That's a bit of a problem, George,' said his wife. 'Jane doesn't *have* much in the way of clothes right at this moment.'

Max Brigstock was persuaded to sit down and drink coffee while Daisy went off to find something for Jane to wear, and presently Jane returned downstairs wearing an old tennis shirt of Ben's and a pair of white shorts Daisy could no longer get into.

Her father eyed the length of exposed brown thigh with doubt. 'I suppose that'll do,' he said grudgingly. 'Better than that shiny pink thing, anyway. Never knew you had such dashing taste in underwear, Daisy.'

As Ben Whitehead glared blackly Mrs Calvert hastily suggested that Jane take Max for a stroll down to the river.

Jane was only too glad to get out of the Whiteheads' kitchen, where the atmosphere, as always when Olivia and George Calvert were together, was a little too electric for comfort. Nevertheless, as Max paced beside her in unbroken silence towards the river bank it occurred to her that she might have jumped out of the frying pan into the fire. They moved out of sight of the house, following a path which led to a decaying little jetty with a wooden bench where Jane sat down, lifting her face to the sun.

'Won't you join me?' she said politely.

Max shook his head. He looked tired and rather drawn in the strong light, and all too obviously impatient to get away.

'No, thanks. Since the sole reason for our tête-à-tête is the expected apology, I'll stay on my feet.'

'How disappointing.' Jane stared out across the sun-dappled water. 'I had such hopes of seeing you on your knees, grovelling.'

'You're honest!'

To Jane's surprise Max changed his mind and sat beside her, his booted feet stretched out in front of him.

'You're well within your rights, I suppose,' he went on heavily. 'Smoke, fright, shock—you name it, all of it must have affected my brain last night. In the cold light of day, even before the blasted inspection, I knew perfectly well that you weren't responsible for the fire.'

Jane shot a sidelong glance at him, surprised. 'Really? You sang a different tune last night.'

Max returned her look so steadily that Jane could see the green flecks in his hazel irises. He ran a hand through his untidy black hair, his mouth turning down at the corners. 'It was all pretty chaotic last night—for one thing I got a hell of a fright when I saw the cottage going up in smoke and thought that you and your mother were inside. It was an enormous relief to find it empty. Then when your mother turned up and said that you had to be in there after all——' He grimaced. 'The stuff night-mares are made of.'

'Why should you have cared?' asked Jane curiously.

'Is it so impossible to believe that I quailed at the thought of another human being asphyxiated in there—even burning to death?' The glitter in his eyes turned to ice. 'Obviously it is. Be that as it may, the result was abnormally irrational behaviour on my part, and I apologise humbly for ever entertaining thoughts of arson in connection with you, Miss Calvert, even for a moment.' He jumped up, looking at his watch. 'There. I hope that will do, because it's high time I was off.'

'Thank you,' said Jane quietly as she got to her feet.

He eyed her warily. 'For what?'

'For taking the trouble to come round and tell us what caused the fire. I know how busy you must be. You could perfectly well have sent your Mr Collins.'

'I would have, believe me, but I could hardly ask him to apologise to you on my behalf,' he said with irony.

'Nevertheless, I appreciate it,' she said firmly, then paused, wondering how to phrase what she wanted to say. 'Perhaps we ought to strike last night from the record, one way and another,' she said awkwardly at last, her eyes falling from the blank astonishment in his. 'Looking back on it you weren't the only one affected by smoke and fright, Mr Brigstock. I was by no means my usual self, either.'

Max looked at her speculatively. 'It would be interesting to learn just exactly what your usual self *is*, you know. Up to now we've met in circumstances which hardly lend themselves to normality—including the evening your vengeful fiancé put in an appearance. Although by then you were a damn sight friendlier than the night of the Whiteheads' party.'

Jane gave him a sudden, cheeky grin which made him blink. 'You weren't supposed to be there, you know.'

His look of blank shock sent her into peals of laughter and eventually, reluctantly, the infectious sound brought a grin to his face in response.

'But I was invited!' he assured her.

'Oh, yes, I know.' Still chuckling, Jane told him how the original party had been planned as a pre-wedding get-together of friends and neighbours, then cancelled due to the last-minute change of plan.

'I was coaxed to go along for dinner just the same because Daisy's my godmother, and she was insistent that I shouldn't brood at home,' she told him, her eyes dancing. 'The trouble was, I gather, that Daisy thought Ben had rung you to cancel and Ben thought *she* had.'

Max winced. 'You must have been pretty appalled—all of you—when I turned up.' He shook his head. 'Full marks to the Whiteheads; I never suspected a thing. I'll admit that it was a bit of a shock to come face to face with you after our run-in that morning, but otherwise I assumed that I was being admitted—at last—into the charmed circle of Wyndcombe hospitality.'

Something in his voice made Jane eye him thoughtfully. 'I gather it was your first essay into local society.'

He nodded. 'I'm regarded as a bit of a Johnny-come-lately. My riches are a bit too *nouveaux* and all that. Funny, really. I anticipated difficulty in being accepted socially, but assumed that my origins in Pipers Flats would be the stumbling block, not my money.' Max looked at his watch again, plainly regretting having said so much. 'And this time I really must go.'

'Should you be in London?'

'No. For the time being Phoenix House is my head-quarters—and at this very moment I've got an architect and a building contractor heaping curses on my head for holding them up.' Max hesitated, then held out a grimy hand. 'Goodbye, then—Miss Calvert. May I take it we've declared a truce?'

Jane nodded. 'Yes. Only I thought it had been de-cided that you were to call me Jane.'

'Ah, yes. Plain Jane.' Max Brigstock took a long, un-hurried look at the girl standing at the water's edge, at the hair shining like liquid honey in the sunlight, shape outlined faithfully by the clinging cotton knit of the shirt, long slim legs below the borrowed shorts. As his eyes reached Jane's face she smiled ruefully.

'I know, I know! I'm well aware that my borrowed plumes don't do very much for me.'

Max smiled back, in a way which took Jane's breath away. 'I can't honestly say that I agree with you there. Which isn't surprising,' he added, with a gleam in his eye. 'Agreement hasn't been a feature of our brief en-counters to date!'

Deliberate charm from Max Brigstock was something that Jane found strangely difficult to cope with, and to disguise the fact she shook his proffered hand in what she hoped was a hearty, jolly-hockey-sticks sort of manner.

'Very true. So truce it is, then.'

Max held on to her hand. 'By the way, I forgot to say that there's no reason why you and your mother can't move into Pond House immediately, if you like—if you can put up with living with decorators for a while.'

Jane took her hand away gently, in case he discovered how madly her pulse was racing. 'I'm still puzzled, you know,' she said slowly.

'What about?'

'Why you are doing all this for my mother. You don't have to. Dower Cottage belongs to you and the lease is up. You're not obliged to provide other accommodation for her at all, are you?' Jane gazed at the dark face questioningly, but Max Brigstock merely shrugged.

'I have my reasons. Some day it's possible that I'll tell you what they are. In the meantime I'd be very grateful if you'd make my apologies to your people and the Whiteheads and say I had to run. Goodbye—Jane.'

'Goodbye—Max,' she added, as he waited pointedly, and he smiled in the same unsettling way again, then took her completely by surprise by bending swiftly to kiss her cheek before setting off at a run for the garden gate, glancing at his watch as he went.

CHAPTER SIX

JANE was on the point of leaving Kilvaraigh when the letter came. Her holiday at the Rintouls' farm had gone by like lightning, all her energy channelled into keeping up with Geordie and Iain, her exuberant little nephews, helping Alastair with his paperwork, and relieving Phillida of any task she could think of when it was proudly announced that a third little Rintoul was expected the coming winter.

After the fire at Dower Cottage Olivia Calvert had surprised herself and everyone else by agreeing to her husband's suggestion of a Caribbean cruise together, to help her recover from the trauma of the fire. So, since Jane was without a base until Pond House was ready, Phillida had insisted that she make the long-promised journey to Kilvaraigh at once for a holiday before embarking on the task of job-hunting. After three busy, restorative weeks, Jane was actually in the car with Phillida, heading for Inverness and the train home, when the postman flagged them down on the narrow cart track to the main road, announcing that he had a letter for Miss Calvert among the mail for Kilvaraigh.

Jane glanced at her typewritten name and the London postmark, thrust it in her bag and forgot it as she lectured Phillida on taking life easy until the new baby was born. Jane was some miles into the journey before she thought of the letter again, and found to her astonishment that it was from Max Brigstock, stating that the decorations and repairs to Pond House were complete. If she wished to move in before her mother's return to

England, Jane was informed, she could do so at any time.

Then came a paragraph which shot Jane's eyebrows into her sun-streaked hair.

'I shall be at Phoenix House when you return from Scotland,' concluded Max, 'and would be very pleased if you would contact me when you arrive, regarding a mutually convenient meeting to clear up a few minor details.'

Jane folded the letter thoughtfully, vastly curious about the 'minor details', wondering what could be important enough to merit a meeting between two people who, to date, had rarely managed to remain civil to each other for more than five minutes at a time, despite occasional lapses into something slightly warmer which were annoyingly difficult to forget.

Jane's immediate goal on her return to Wyndcombe was the Whiteheads' house. She had intended spending only the weekend there before going off to London to stay with a friend while she went job-hunting, but now that Pond House was ready it seemed a wonderful idea to organise the move at once and simply have everything ready and waiting as a surprise for her mother when she got home. Jane's eyes danced as she thought that her mother might well be glad of a rest after nearly a month spent in company with George Calvert!

Ben and Daisy Whitehead met Jane at the station, exclaiming on her tan and demanding details of her holiday, and Jane put all thoughts of her letter out of her mind until much later that evening, when the telephone rang during dinner and Ben returned to the dining-room to say that Max Brigstock wanted a word with Jane. Grinning at Daisy's unabashed curiosity, Jane went into Ben's study and picked up the telephone.

'Hello. Jane here.'

'Good evening. How was your holiday?'

'Very enjoyable. I received your letter this morning, by the way,' Jane added.

'Ah, good. Apropos of my request, then, could we meet tomorrow, by any chance? I'm away most of next week.'

'Fine. When do you suggest?'

There was a short silence. 'I'm tied up most of the day,' said Max slowly.

On a *Sunday*? thought Jane. Doesn't the man ever let up?

'Would it be possible for you to join me for dinner?' he went on.

'You mean, you don't work right through your meals as well?' Jane couldn't resist saying.

'I do; often. But not if a better alternative presents itself.'

'My company being marginally preferable to a bundle of plans, you mean!'

'A better way to phrase that escapes me for the moment. So, Miss Jane Calvert, may I take it that I shall have the pleasure of your company tomorrow at eight?'

Why not? thought Jane. 'Yes, thank you. I'll see you then. Goodnight.'

Sunday was dull and wet all day, even chilly as Jane went off to change for her evening at Phoenix House. She found that she was quite looking forward to it, eager to see the fabled improvements Max Brigstock was said to have made to the old house. And she was not averse to breaking bread with the enemy, either, if it resulted in a quick move into Pond House. Not, Jane realised, that she thought of Max Brigstock as the enemy quite so much since their conversation by the river. Probably, she decided, because her trip to Scotland had done wonders in restoring her to her normal, rational self, particularly with regard to Dower Cottage. As she dressed in Daisy's guest room, she wondered how the cottage was getting along. According to Ben swarms of people had been working on it ever since the fire: thatchers, joiners, electricians, painters. Max Brigstock was pulling out all the stops to restore the place to its former glory at top speed, it seemed.

After the unexpectedly fine weather of her holiday in Scotland the evening felt cool. Jane regretfully abandoned any idea of showing off her tan. Most of her clothes had survived their visit to the cleaners' very well, so she chose the type of outfit she'd worn for work on special days: a cream, lace-trimmed linen blouse and a swirling, chiffon-fine paisley wool skirt printed in biscuit and cream on black and worn with a cropped black cashmere jacket and black suede shoes. She hung pearls from her earlobes, brushed her hair to hang in its usual smooth order just clear of her shoulders, sprayed herself with perfume, then ran down to say goodbye to Daisy and Ben, who provided her with a key in case they happened to be in bed when she got back.

Jane took the road which avoided Dower Cottage as she drove to Phoenix House. She had decided, quite soon after the fire, that the best way to get over her obsession with her old home was to avoid it entirely for the time being, until, in fact, someone else was living in it and had put their own personal stamp on the place. Then she forgot the cottage as she came in sight of Phoenix House, struck once more by the subtlety of the restoration. Outside it looked as it must have done long ago, before Olivia Verney Calvert had even been born. Inside, Jane found, it was a different story.

'Mr Brigstock's been delayed by an urgent phone call,' apologised Liz Collins as she led Jane through the hall, which was painted in the dull coral shade Jane associated with the great houses her father had taken her to as a child to look at the paintings. George Calvert would approve of only some of Max Brigstock's taste in art, thought Jane, as she passed a series of landscapes and watercolours on her way to the small room once reserved for her grandmother's use, and which was now, it seemed, the place where Max Brigstock relaxed. If he ever did.

Unlike the formality of the hall, the morning-room was furnished for comfort, with big, masculine chairs upholstered in dark blue cord, a chesterfield covered in rubbed tan leather, and Sunday papers and a tray of drinks on the handsome sofa-table behind it. This was a man's room, with no cushions or bits and pieces, the long windows hung with plain, natural linen bordered with a Greek key design in dark blue.

'Attractive,' commented Jane.

Mrs Collins smiled. 'Mr Brigstock's taste, this room.'

'Not the rest of the house?'

'Not exactly, Miss Calvert. What may I get you to drink? Mr Brigstock won't be a moment.'

Deciding to keep to a glass of mineral water, Jane wandered over to the windows once she was alone, and looked out on gardens in such perfect order that she wondered how many staff were necessary to achieve it. Even on a dull grey evening, as now, the vista was a delight to the eye, with conifer and beech and Japanese maple framing a lawn which stretched like green velvet to the walls hiding the pool Max had built in the old sunken garden.

'You approve?' said a quiet voice, and Jane swung round, smiling, as Max Brigstock came to join her, looking elegant in a dark blue suit with a silk shirt the same ivory colour as the dots patterning his dark blue foulard tie. He looked a great deal less tense than on their previous couple of encounters; tanned and rested and very, very attractive indeed, thought Jane with a sense of shock. Was the old saw right, after all? Maybe absence really did make the heart grow, if not fonder precisely, certainly somewhat warmer as far as Max Brigstock was concerned. She held out her hand.

'How do you do? And yes, I do approve. Well, mostly.'

Max clasped her hand briefly, then went over to the tray to pour himself a small Scotch before joining her at the window. 'I'm curious. Why is your approval qualified?'

Jane eyed him searchingly, trying to assess his mood, but as usual his face gave no clue to the thoughts behind it. 'I'm trying very hard not to offend, you understand, but for my particular taste it's all a shade too perfect. Probably,' she added hastily, 'because I remember it as it was before—a sort of elegant shambles.'

She relaxed as Max grinned.

'I remember it that way, too. I used to do some very illicit fishing on the stretch of river running through Verney land—which is how it's known to this day in Pipers Flats, you'll be pleased to hear.'

'Did you catch much?'

'A couple now and then—and a good hiding for poaching, into the bargain. Not that family scruples prevented grilled trout from appearing for the next meal.' Something in Max's smile touched a chord in Jane.

'Was your childhood unhappy?' she asked impulsively, then bit her lip. 'Sorry. I don't mean to pry.'

Max's face softened. 'You don't have to watch your "p"s and "q"s with me all the time, you know. I don't offend that easily.'

Jane raised a doubting eyebrow. 'No? I rather thought I'd managed it *very* easily every time we've met—so far.'

He grinned again, looking younger and less formidable as he took her glass to refill it. 'Perhaps tonight will mark a different phase in our acquaintance.' He raised his own glass in salute. 'To *détente*, Jane.'

'To *détente*!' she echoed, and gave him a smile which elicited a very unexpected response.

'No wonder poor Fry was in such a state,' Max said, shaking his head. 'Quite a blow for the poor chap, to find himself jilted at the last minute by a girl like you.'

Jane eyed him quizzically. 'A girl like me?'

Max nodded, and waved a hand towards the sofa. 'Won't you sit down? Dinner won't be long.'

Jane chose one of the deep blue chairs and put her glass very carefully on the small pedestal table beside it. Max remained standing, leaning an elbow on the marble mantel above the fireplace.

'I was, if you can bring yourself to believe it, trying to pay you a compliment,' he said, so poker-faced that Jane chuckled.

'I'm glad you told me—I'd *never* have guessed!'

'I'm no expert at compliments, I'm afraid.'

'Since you're expert in so many other fields, I don't suppose that it worries you much,' said Jane lightly.

Max was quiet for a moment, regarding her thoughtfully. 'Would you consider *me* guilty of prying, as you call it, if I confessed to curiosity about why you changed your mind?'

Jane looked at him levelly. 'No, I don't think so. You don't strike me as a man interested in idle gossip.' She was silent for a moment, very much aware of his intent, bright gaze, then, dispassionately as possible, she gave him a pared-down account of the brief nature of her relationship with Adrian, of the research post which had accelerated their wedding plans, then, even though she'd given up her job and her flat, her guilty realisation that marriage was out of the question.

'Entirely?' asked Max casually.

'Yes, as far as Adrian's concerned.' Jane smiled wryly. 'And since I'm not exactly besieged at the moment by— by——'

'Replacements for him?' he suggested blandly.

Jane's lips twitched. 'Not the way I'd have put it. Let's just say that matrimony seems to have receded into the dim and distant future—infinity, even.'

'Do you regret that?'

'As far as being a wife and mother in general terms, yes. But from the viewpoint of being Mrs Adrian Fry, no. I blame myself bitterly for not realising how ill-suited we were a great deal earlier, before marriage was even considered. Adrian's really a very nice man. He didn't deserve the treatment I gave him.'

A knock on the door interrupted them, as Liz Collins announced dinner.

The dining-room was a different kettle of fish from the casual comfort of Max's private sanctum. Here all was formality, with a genuine Georgian table big enough for a board meeting, chairs upholstered in the heavy striped silk of the swagged, fringed curtains at the windows, hunting scenes shoulder to shoulder on the panelled walls and quantities of valuable silver on the sideboards. Slightly oppressed by it all, Jane felt far greater enthusiasm for the food, which was of a very high standard indeed.

'Liz is a trained chef,' said Max, as Jane exclaimed over lobster mousse in an exquisite saffron sauce.

'Mrs Collins, you're a genius,' she said, as Liz replaced the first course with tournedos of beef. The young woman gave Jane a shy smile of gratitude, then bade them both goodnight as she left them to their dinner.

'That was very nice of you,' said Max warmly.

Jane smiled a little as she helped herself from an impressive array of fresh vegetables. 'Does the fact that I can be "nice", as you put it, surprise you so much?'

He shook his head, his eyes gleaming with mock contrition. 'I told you I'm no good at compliments!'

Then with a smoothness which belied his professed lack of social graces Max questioned Jane about her holiday, listening, amused, as she described her attempts at milking Alastair's cows, the fun she'd had playing with her energetic little nephews. While they ate the exquisite food, and enjoyed the cheese and fresh fruit which followed it, their pleasure in each other's company was a factor which neither of them even attempted to hide.

At Jane's request Max spoke of the work he was engaged in at Pipers Flats, waxing quietly eloquent on his aim of providing a miniature model village, where neighbours could enjoy reasonable proximity to each other without being crammed into plots so small that privacy was impossible.

'It's by no means new,' he assured her. 'Viscount Leverhulme achieved it with great success at Port Sunlight as far back as 1881.'

Jane listened, absorbed, as he went on to describe the design that he'd approved for the houses to be built at Pipers Flats. With an animation on his hard features which transformed them rather startlingly, he told her that his aim was a direct relationship to the natural environment, with an overall design influenced by the rurality of the location and proximity to the river, and, importantly, use of local materials wherever possible.

'Would you consider me very fanciful,' he said later, as Jane presided over a coffee tray in the morning-room, 'if I said that early on in my career I took to heart something once said by St Catherine of Siena, about the city being the image of the soul. Only in my case I do my best to apply it in a rural as well as urban context.'

Jane, far from considering him fanciful, was in total sympathy, and would have questioned Max further, except that she realised that time was passing and so far Pond House had not been mentioned. Reluctantly, she changed the subject to ask if it would be possible to move in before her mother returned.

'As soon as you like.' Max gave her a wry smile. 'I hope it won't disturb this new-found amity between us when you learn that I've taken it on myself to have some of your mother's things moved there already. A lot of it needed attention of one kind or another,' he went on hastily, at her look of surprise. 'And with all the work going on at Dower Cottage it seemed best to get your mother's belongings out of the way once they were cleaned or restored, rather than risk further damage.'

'When you say "some",' said Jane delicately, 'what, exactly, do you mean?'

'Well, everything, really. The only room totally empty is yours.' Max's smile was conciliatory. 'Since all your belongings went up in smoke your mother wanted you to choose new things yourself.' He asked permission to smoke a cigar, then returned to his post at the fireplace as he surprised Jane by informing her that it had all been done with approval from both Olivia *and* George Calvert.

In the short period between Jane's departure for Scotland and her parents' for their cruise in the Caribbean, Max Brigstock, it seemed, had seen quite a bit of the Calverts for necessary consultation. Jane was taken aback to learn that the two men had got on surprising well together, George Calvert professing himself in total accord with Max Brigstock's style of property development.

'After the—er—slight awkwardness of our first meeting I found that your father and I have quite a lot in common,' said Max, lips twitching.

'You astound me,' said Jane, laughing. 'My father usually manages to tread on every toe in his vicinity.'

'A forceful personality!'

The small French clock on the marble mantel struck eleven, bringing Jane to her feet. 'Heavens, I must go. I had no idea it was so late.'

'Will the Whiteheads be waiting up for you?'

'No, but——'

'Then won't you please stay a little longer? I haven't even touched on the main reason for asking you here tonight.'

Jane's eyebrows rose. 'I thought it was to discuss Pond House!'

Max smiled slightly. 'Shall we say I used Pond House as my excuse.'

'I don't understand.'

'If you'll sit down again for a moment, I'll explain.'

Jane did as he asked, feeling baffled. Up to now their common interest had centred, with notable lack of harmony on occasion, on Dower Cottage. Now that that particular bone of contention was disposed of, and Pond House ready for occupation, she wondered what they had in common which could remotely merit serious discussion. Unless one counted the growing rapport between them, and that, she told herself sternly, might be something she was imagining, rather than an established fact.

'I'm very interested to know what you have in mind,' began Max with care, 'with regard to your future.'

Jane just managed to prevent her jaw from dropping in astonishment. 'Why?' she asked baldly.

'I've a perfectly logical reason for asking, I promise.'

Jane shrugged. 'Nothing very different from what I did in the past, I suppose. My immediate aim is to get Mother settled at Pond House when she gets home, then I'm off to London, job-hunting. I sold my flat, as you know, but hopefully it shouldn't be too difficult to find somewhere else to live.'

Max eyed her questioningly. 'How do you feel about a job in a more rural setting?'

Jane sternly controlled the jubilant little leap her heart performed beneath the linen and lace and cashmere. 'Do you know of one, then?'

'Yes. Here at Phoenix House.' Max looked rather tense, Jane thought, as he went on to explain that for some time into the foreseeable future he would be spending a proportion of his time in Wyndcombe while the development of Pipers Flats was in progress. 'This means that I need someone competent and reliable to work for me here in Wyndcombe,' he went on. 'An assistant capable of holding the fort whether I'm here or not—so I thought of you. Miss Jane Calvert; no stranger to responsibility, with good business training and proven experience in handling the public.'

'How do you know all that?'

'I made it my business to find out.'

Jane's hackles rose instinctively at this but she ignored any slight resentment at his high-handedness, aware that it would hardly be sensible to throw away what looked, even at first glance, like a golden opportunity. 'What would I be expected to do?' she asked at last.

'I don't know what your former job entailed exactly, of course,' said Max impersonally, 'but working for me would mean dealing with a certain amount of correspondence, the odd report. I assume that you have the usual office skills, even if they're a bit rusty. But mainly I need someone to liaise for me. Someone, moreover, who sounds not only efficient and charming over the phone, but who's capable of holding her own with local contractors and so on when the going gets rough. As it often does,' he added.

'I see,' said Jane neutrally, secretly rather elated to learn that Max Brigstock was actually offering her a job.

'There is something else,' Max added, with a note of constraint. 'I think I should make it plain that the very fact of who and what you are is why I'm offering you the job.'

Jane thought that one over at some length. 'Well, I know *who* I am, of course,' she said eventually. 'But I'm a little in the dark about *what* I am from your point of view.'

Max got to his feet and offered her a brandy, which she refused. He strolled over to the drinks tray and poured some for himself; rather, thought Jane, surprised, as though he needed fortifying.

'You are Miss Jane Calvert,' began Max, and for a moment paused, as though this were explanation enough. Then he turned to look at her, his eyes gleaming under half-closed lids. 'Your family once lived here in this house, you grew up in the village of Wyndcombe, went away to an expensive girls' school, then, rather surprisingly for someone like you, made a success of a business career in the City.'

'An exemplary record,' agreed Jane tartly. 'Pity I blotted my hitherto pristine copybook just recently!'

'Only slightly. Not nearly enough to mar the overall picture. Let me show you what I mean.'

Mystified, Jane followed Max's tall figure into the hall, where twin mirrors hung opposite each other, framed with gilded Victorian extravagance. Obediently she stood in front of one of them alongside Max.

'What do you see?' he asked.

Jane studied their reflections; her own, glowing from its breath of fresh Scottish air, groomed and quietly elegant, in the type of clothes she knew suited her best. In contrast Max's saturnine face looked darker than usual over her shoulder, his reflected eyes intently gold as a tiger's.

'I see you and me,' stated Jane, wondering what he wanted to hear.

'Shall I tell you what *I* see?' he said softly. 'Behind you stands a successful man dressed in expensive, custom-made clothes. But inside them he's still the boy from Pipers Flats.' His eyes held hers in the mirror. 'Whereas you look exactly what you are and always have been—the product of a secure and privileged background; the way you dress, the way you speak, your supreme confidence in your own place in things.'

Jane turned away from the mirror to face him. 'Tell me something. Are you ashamed of coming from Pipers Flats?'

'On the contrary. I'm damn proud of it. What I am, what I have, I achieved for myself.' The twist of his lips was cynical. 'And until I bought this house it wasn't something I even thought of. In London I'm respected for my acumen, for my vision—and, most of all, my capacity for making money. But here in Wyndcombe I'm the outsider who's had the nerve not only to take up residence in Verney House but to lash out money on it in a way which apparently puts him beyond the pale of local society.'

'So what do you want *me* to do, then?' asked Jane, as they went back to the morning-room.'

'Come and work for me. I meant what I said. But I should make it clear that I need the services of an assistant who is not only competent, but must be prepared to act as——' Max paused. 'I don't quite know how to phrase it, without giving offence, but the word which presents itself is "hostess".'

'You mean organise dinner-parties, perhaps, that sort of thing?' ventured Jane, eyeing him.

'Not only organise them, Miss Calvert, but preside over them. It wouldn't be necessary very often,' he added. 'I'm not a social animal. Shall we just say that

I have a fancy to show the residents of Wyndcombe that the stranger in their midst is not a total upstart.'

Jane flushed bright red, and his straight brows knitted.

'What have I said?'

'I thought you were quoting.'

'You mean you've used the term yourself!'

'And a few far less acceptable, I'm afraid, after you accused me of arson.'

They regarded each other steadily for a moment, then Jane's warm, friendly smile spread from her eyes to the full curves of her mouth, and Max smiled involuntarily in response.

'Well?' he asked. 'Will you accept the offer?'

'Will you give me time to think about it?'

'Very well.' Max shot back his shirt cuff to consult his watch. 'Today is the twenty-eighth. I'd need to know by the thirtieth, please, so that I can get on with finding someone else if you refuse.'

'Do you usually give prospective employees such leeway?'

He smiled. 'Never. But then, I rarely interview employees myself these days. I pay people to do it for me.'

'Why the exception in my case?'

'Merely because circumstances dictated it—and I'm giving you time to think it over because I assume that you had no idea a job was what I had in mind when I asked you here tonight.'

Jane shook her head. 'None at all. You just said "minor details" in your letter. A job may be a minor detail to you, of course, but to me at the moment it looms rather large on my particular horizon.'

'Then I hope you'll look on my suggestion with approval,' said Max promptly. 'In the meantime, would you care to see what's been done in some of the other rooms?'

'I would, very much,' said Jane at once, hoping her curiosity wasn't too blatantly obvious as she jumped smartly to her feet to follow Max from the room.

As a child Jane had been allowed to play occasionally in the grounds of her mother's one-time home but had rarely ventured inside the house, which by then had become a home for the elderly, and therefore to the young Jane very intimidating. Now the contrast was so enormous that it took her breath away.

The drawing-room Max showed her seemed vaster than her memory of it, furnished in Louis XIV style, with a great deal of ormolu and gilt, and a magnificent Aubusson carpet. Gilded chandeliers hung from the ceiling, and the huge marble fireplace, though ancient itself, Max informed a rather silent Jane, was new to the house, taken from a Scottish castle.

'With the owners' consent, of course,' he added, a glint in his eye as he led the way to his study which, after the opulence of the drawing-room, was functional and rather bleak in its electronically equipped perfection. Next door was a small, elegant room which had once been the province of the housekeeper but would now, Jane learned, become her own particular domain if she accepted the job. Beyond it lay the conservatory which Jane remembered as a dilapidated place with cracked, dusty glass and tired palms, but which now gleamed in unbroken perfection, filled with exotic plant life unfamiliar not only to Jane, to her amusement, but also to Max, who confessed that he left the horticultural side of things to the frightening old man who worked with a team of local lads to keep the grounds in such perfect order.

'Well?' he said, as they returned to the morning-room. 'What do you think of my house?'

'Did you choose it all yourself?'

'Good grief, no. I never have the time.' He waved a hand about him. 'I brought most of this stuff from my London place, but the rest of the house was done by a firm of interior decorators.'

Jane nodded, unsurprised. 'Very impressive.' She picked up her handbag, then held out her hand. 'Thank you for dinner. It was quite wonderful. Please tell Mrs Collins I said so.'

Max took her hand in his, holding it for a moment as he looked into the clear, amber eyes not so very far below his own. 'Thank you for coming. I've enjoyed the evening.'

'So have I.'

'You sound surprised.'

'I am,' said Jane honestly. 'Frankly, it seemed unlikely that we could spend an entire evening in each other's company without coming to blows.'

'Whereas the behaviour's been exemplary—on both sides.' He held open one of the tall windows leading out on to the terrace, then walked with her to the car. 'I'll be away until fairly late on the evening of the thirtieth. I shall hope to hear from you on my return. In the meantime Jim Collins will give you any help you want when you move into Pond House.'

Jane got into the car and opened the window to lean out. 'I haven't thanked you enough for organising all that, you know. I feel very much in your debt.'

Max Brigstock smiled persuasively. 'Come and work for me and I'll consider it paid in full.'

Jane was tempted to agree there and then, but something told her that Max Brigstock would appreciate her acceptance far more if she took time to consider it, so she gave him a friendly smile, said goodnight, then drove back to Wyndcombe in a very preoccupied mood indeed.

CHAPTER SEVEN

'YOU both look wonderful!' cried Jane as she tried to hug both her tanned parents at once at Heathrow two days later. She held her mother at arm's length, over-joyed to see Olivia Calvert looking rested and fit and remarkably youthful. George Calvert, as always, looked larger than life in a creased white linen suit and outsize panama hat as he tossed suitcases into Jane's car, thrust Olivia inside it, then surprised his daughter by kissing her goodbye.

'Goodbye!' echoed Jane, dismayed.

'Your father's off to his place for a day or two,' said Mrs Calvert placidly, and held up a cheek in turn for a kiss.

Jane stared, open-mouthed. Demonstrations of af-fection between her parents were rare.

'Things to see to,' said George Calvert briskly. 'Your mother will explain. Off, off—you're parked illegally, child.'

Olivia Calvert chuckled as Jane had no option but to move off into the traffic, leaving her father to duck into a waiting taxi. 'Don't look so disappointed, Jane. He's got a few things to see to in town, then he's coming down to Wyndcombe for a bit.'

Jane could hardly believe her ears. She begged her mother to explain, almost crashing into the car in front when she learned that her parents had decided to try living together again for an experimental period. Their holiday had proved, against all odds, to be not only a success, but the major factor in effecting a reconciliation.

'Are you pleased?' asked Mrs Calvert.

Since Jane's radiant smile was answer enough, Olivia went on to demand all her daughter's news in return, and was so engrossed in it that she failed to notice that they were making for Pond House until Jane parked the car in the drive, and Daisy and Ben came hurrying out to meet them.

It was much later that evening, after supper had been eaten and the Whiteheads had gone home, and mother and daughter were drinking coffee near the open french windows of their new sitting-room, when Jane asked the only question left unanswered.

'Mother,' she began tentatively. 'Harking back to my future plans, would you mind very much if I lived at home for a while?'

'Of course, not, darling.' Olivia Calvert's eyes lingered with pleasure on her daughter's lounging figure, graceful even in faded old jeans and madras shirt.

'The thing is, I've been offered a job here.'

'Here?'

'Yes. Max Brigstock needs a PA here in Wyndcombe—for the time being, anyway, while he's involved in the Pipers Flats project. He's going to be dashing back and forth between here and the City, apparently, which means that he needs someone who can cope with this end of things on her own. So he asked me if I'd like the job.'

'Max Brigstock!' breathed Mrs Calvert, dumbfounded. 'Good lord, Jane—a bit of a turn-up for the books. What did you say?'

'Not much. I haven't actually accepted yet. I was waiting for you to get back. But I'm supposed to give him his answer tonight.' Jane dropped on her knees beside her mother. 'What do you think?'

Mrs Calvert quite plainly wasn't sure what to think. 'It's a bit of a bombshell, really. Will you be *able* to work for him? Without fighting, I mean?'

'Oh, I'm all over that now,' Jane assured her airily, not ready yet to admit how differently she'd felt towards Max Brigstock of late. 'Besides, Max has been pretty generous over this place, hasn't he? I can hardly go on wailing about Dower Cottage under the circumstances.'

'So he's "Max" now! Whatever happened to "the upstart"?'

Jane grinned, and startled her mother even further by giving an account of her evening at Phoenix House.

Mrs Calvert shook her head, amazed. 'Wonders never cease! Goodness, don't keep me in suspense. What does it look like now that he's had it done over?'

'On the whole a bit formal and grand for my taste—but never mind that now.' Jane eyed her mother questioningly. 'I want to know what you think, Mother. Shall I take the job or not?'

'I think you've already made up your mind.' Olivia Calvert smiled slyly at her daughter. 'Haven't you?'

Jane nodded sheepishly. 'I'll admit it would be rather nice to get out of London for a while. And the job Max is offering sounds just my cup of tea.'

'Then what's your problem? Accept it, child!'

'If I do, could I bag the big attic-room on the top floor——?' Jane hesitated. 'Or does Dad want that for a studio?'

'He's not being offered it,' said Olivia drily. 'He, too, intends to divide himself pro tem between London and Wyndcombe, and fancies doing up a barn, or something, as his country studio. He also wants to buy Pond House from Max for me, but I feel it's early days to go burning all *my* boats quite yet.'

Jane gave a whistle of disbelief. 'I can hardly believe all this. Will it last, Mother?'

Olivia nodded serenely. 'I think it may, you know. Your father has finally come to realise that he's mortal, just like the rest of us. Hence the urge to remain permanently in the bosom of his family.'

'Is that what *you* want, Mother?'

Olivia Calvert's smile was oddly girlish. 'Yes, I find it is. George is still George, of course, but he's changed lately. The possibility that you and I could have perished in the fire at Dower Cottage seems to have had a profound effect on him.'

'In which case it was a blessing in disguise, not the disaster I made such a fuss about!' Jane looked at the clock. 'Max Brigstock's probably back by now. Time I gave him the glad news.'

Max's voice, even at the other end of a telephone line, held an audible note of triumph when Jane informed him that she would like the job he offered.

'I'm very pleased,' he said, with such emphasis that she was taken aback.

'I hope you still feel that way after I've been working for you for a while,' she retorted.

'How could I fail to be pleased, when I shall have Miss Jane Calvert at my beck and call all day?'

Jane eyed the receiver askance. 'I'm not sure I like the sound of that.'

'Don't worry—I'll be the soul of kindness as a boss, no whips and flails, nary a harsh word!'

'Mr Brigstock, sir, are you by any chance inebriated?'

'Only by the thought of having you work for me, Jane, I assure you!'

In a remarkably short time Jane felt as though she'd been working at Phoenix House for years. Max Brigstock was, as promised, a lenient employer most of the time: courteous, decisive, with a flattering tendency to regard Jane as equal to anything the job might demand of her; and, once she'd familiarised herself with all the latest technological gadgets he provided for her use, Jane decided that she'd made the right move. She found the work different, but stimulating, and enjoyed her involvement with the Pipers Flats project as she sat in on meetings with all types of people, from architects to building contractors.

She had been working for Max Brigstock for almost a month before she came up against a side of him very new to her. While there had been no further steps towards a more intimate relationship, Jane nevertheless felt serenely convinced that Max was merely biding his time on this score until she was firmly established as part of his workforce, and basked in his whole-hearted approval as his assistant on the Pipers Flats project after only a week or two. Which made it all the more mortifying when she ran up against his opposition in no uncertain manner on the subject of the various landscape gardeners tendering for his pet project. Jane was all for giving the contract to a local firm who, although unable to tender the lowest figure for the job, was, she firmly believed, most sympathetic in its aims for the final finished look of the development at Pipers Flats.

'I disagree, Jane,' said Max bluntly.

It was late, on a day which had been sultry and threatening since early morning, and the heavy atmosphere added to the tension which crackled in the air between them as Jane argued the case for the local firm.

'Think of the good-will you'll earn locally,' she said persuasively, 'if you give the contract to the Brownlows.'

'Jane,' said Max acidly, 'I haven't got where I am today by putting local good-will at the top of my priorities, and two of the other firms quote a damn sight lower than your precious Brownlows.'

'Money isn't everything!'

'The classic remark from someone who's never felt the lack of it,' he snapped. 'Write to County Landscapes

accepting their tender, and send off refusals to the rest—
including the Brownlows.'

Jane stared at him balefully. 'And all because of a few
miserable pennies! I feel terrible—I went to school with
Melissa Brownlow.'

Max looked at her with eyes as cold as green-veined
ice. 'It is those pennies you are denigrating which go to
pay your salary, Miss Jane Calvert, which leads me on
quite neatly to remind you that you are my employee
and that I give the orders. The "old-boy"—or in this
case "old-girl"—system doesn't work in my outfit. I've
chosen County Landscapes because they not only tender
the best price, but I also prefer the work they do to your
precious Brownlows, who are not only expensive, but
also notorious locally for not completing a job in the
time promised. The fact that you went to school with
one of the Brownlow daughters is of no interest at all
to me. It's merit, efficiency and value for money I'm
interested in, from building contractors to the humblest
of secretaries. Like you. Do I make myself clear?'

'Perfectly,' said Jane, frozen-faced. 'Do you wish me
to get the acceptance—and the refusals—off tonight?'

'Yes,' he snapped, and immersed himself in a pile of
work before Jane even left the room.

The incident was a salutary experience. Jane worked
in simmering silence, seething inside with anger, resentment—and disappointment, she realised, humili-
ated. Somehow she had never imagined that Max would
speak to her like that. And yet she should have, she
thought, eyes kindling. What else could one expect from
a man who'd clawed his way to the top by whatever
means he could manage! But she'd begun to think that
she, at least, was someone whose opinion he valued. Yet
he'd brushed it aside in a way which made it clear that
the relationship she'd fondly believed was developing
between them was, if it even existed outside her imagin-

ation, a very separate thing from Max Brigstock's business life. However good she might be at her job, he'd made it crystal-clear that he was the boss and she was expected to remember at all times that she was merely his humble employee.

There was nothing in the least humble about Jane's attitude when she presented her sheaf of letters for Max's signature. His face was expressionless as he signed them in the slashing black scrawl she now knew so well, but as he handed them across to her he eyed Jane's taut face questioningly.

'You're angry still,' he observed.

She inclined her head in agreement and went on folding letters into envelopes.

'Because I disagreed with you, Jane?'

She looked up, her jaw clenching as she saw that his eyes held the mockery which had been missing lately. 'I think I'm angry with myself,' she said carefully.

'Why?'

'Over my unwarranted presumption. I honestly thought that you valued my opinion—in certain matters, anyway.'

'I do. But I reserve the right to stick to my own judgement just the same. I've had a fair amount of experience at it, after all. But if I let you know in an offensive way, I apologise.'

'No need. I'm sure it was necessary.' Jane smiled coldly. 'It's better that I know my place, after all. I'd begun to forget that you crack the whip. My mistake.'

Max leaned back in his chair, frowning. 'I hope this doesn't mean that you want to leave.'

Jane gathered her bundle of letters together. 'Not for the moment, certainly.' She gave him a composed little smile. 'If I'd left my employment after every run-in with male colleagues—even so-called superiors—I'd never have worked for long anywhere, Mr Brigstock, I assure you.'

Jane reported for work next day with some trepidation, but Max Brigstock behaved as though nothing had happened, and after a while it seemed as though nothing had. But though they resumed their usual friendly working relationship, Jane was wary after that of overstepping any employer/employee line she felt that Max might have drawn between them. The odd thing, she found, was that the lecture he'd given her did nothing to damp down her more personal feelings for him. Jane tried hard to ignore the fact that she set off for Phoenix House every day buoyed up by expectation, merely because she was about to spend it in company with Max Brigstock, and sometimes at night took herself to task in the privacy of her room for being a fool. After surviving her recent unhappy experience with Adrian it seemed downright foolhardy to expose herself to the far deeper hurt she knew very well she would feel if she suffered rejection from Max Brigstock.

'All things considered, by which I mean the vagaries of my uncertain temper, are you still able to say that you're enjoying it here?' asked Max one warm evening towards the end of Jane's second month.

'I am, indeed,' Jane was able to say with complete truth.

'And have you all managed to settle down together at Pond House?' Max asked, taking off his jacket.

Jane laughed. 'Reasonably well, though since you're our landlord I think you ought to know that Father took it into his head to decorate my bedroom for me, would you believe? He's actually painted a mural on one wall—brought part of the garden right into the room. It's quite wonderful.'

'I'd like to see it some time——' Max's eyes gleamed suddenly. 'Which, I suppose, considering the mural's precise location, is hardly the right thing to say.'

Jane grinned. 'I hadn't thought of that. I'll be able to say "come up and see my mural", instead of the old chestnut about etchings.'

'I thought that was the man's line!'

'Which doesn't prevent *me* from using it—not,' Jane added, laughing, 'that there's much danger of anything like that with my father around. He's grown exhaustingly protective to his womenfolk since the fire.'

'Understandable.' Max rotated his head on his neck wearily. 'Are you in a hurry to get away?'

'No, not really. Is there something else you'd like me to do?'

'Yes. Have a drink with me out on the terrace.'

Jane looked at him, taken aback. Since their disagreement over the landscaping of Pipers Flats a certain reserve had entered her dealings with Max. But now, as Max looked at her cajolingly, Jane abandoned her dignity and smiled with warmth.

'Thank you. That would be very pleasant.'

She was right. It was. The evening was sunny, and still hot, and the long, cold gin and tonic full of ice and lemon slices was just what she needed as they relaxed in garden chairs to enjoy the sunset.

'Will you want me here tomorrow?' asked Jane drowsily.

'On a *Saturday*?' said Max, his eyes suddenly alight with mockery.

'Please—don't remind me,' said Jane, pulling a face. 'I put my foot in it so thoroughly the first time I came here that I'm amazed you ever even contemplated asking me to work for you.'

'Are you?' said Max cryptically, and stared into his glass. 'Perhaps I've got a forgiving nature.'

'I don't think I believe that, quite.'

'Why not?'

'Something about the way you talked the night I came to dinner gave me the idea that, well, you bear a grudge of some kind towards some of the people round here.' Jane shot a look at him, wondering if she'd put her foot in it again.

Max grinned. 'Worried about those "p"'s and "q"'s?'

'Something like that.'

'Don't be. I don't approve of people who say only what they think I want to hear.'

Jane laughed. 'Highly unlikely, in my case. I'm too much the other way—as you know,' she added significantly.

'None better, I fancy! But you're right, of course. There are certain of Wyndcombe's inhabitants who weren't exactly charitable to the likes of me and my kind in the old days. Are you driving?' Max added suddenly.

'No. In weather like this I walk to work—glad of the exercise.'

'Then have another of these. Unless you have something to rush off to, perhaps?'

Jane shook her head. 'Dad's in London, Mother's playing bridge.'

Max's eyebrows rose as he handed her another drink. 'Is there no one else interested in how you pass your evenings?'

'Not here in Wyndcombe. In London it's different, of course.'

'Do you miss the social life?'

Jane thought for a moment. 'No,' she said slowly. 'At least, not for now. After my recent débâcle I find the restorative powers of the quiet life very much to my taste.'

They were sitting on the balustraded terrace which led, by way of shallow, worn steps, to a croquet lawn bordered by a semi-wild stretch of woodland. This, as Jane

knew from her childhood, was the haunt of badgers with
a passion for rolling on the fragrant blue carpet of blue-
bells under the trees in spring, also for digging holes in
the lawns; pastimes which brought down curses on their
protected heads from Daniels, the gardener. The sun was
low in the sky above the trees, and Jane lay back in her
chair, relaxed as she enjoyed the peaceful prospect before
her.

Max sat as still as Jane, but as always his posture had
a tautness about it, as though to relax were akin to sur-
render of some kind. Jane watched him from the corner
of her eye, wondering how *his* evenings were spent when
he was absent from Phoenix House. Was there someone
in London who featured largely in his social life, cooked
intimate little dinners for him—shared his bed? She felt
a searing pang of jealousy at the thought, and swallowed
half of her drink to hide her dismay at the violence of
her reaction.

'Penny for your thoughts,' said Max and watched, lips
twitching, as colour rose in Jane's face. 'Or perhaps I
should up the price!'

'I was wondering,' said Jane, deciding to risk honesty,
'about *your* social life. Not,' she added hastily, 'that I
expect you to enlarge on it. But—well, you *are* a well-
known figure in the business world; you're single, sought
after, I imagine. Yet I never read about you in the Press.'

'I take damn good care that no one reads about me.'
Max laughed shortly. 'I prefer my private life to remain
just that: private.'

Which, thought Jane, puts me back in my place again.
Why won't I learn? She finished the last of her drink
and stood up. 'Thank you. That was just what I needed.'

Max jumped to his feet and took her hand. 'You're
offended. I'm sorry.'

'I'm not, so don't be.' She smiled at him cheerfully.
'Privacy is a precious commodity. I don't blame you for

conserving it.' She tried, without success, to withdraw
her hand, conscious suddenly of the nearness of Max's
spare, athletic body as he stood closer to her than was
his normal habit.

'Won't you stay and have dinner with me?' he asked,
his eyes suddenly intent.

Sternly controlling the instinct to say yes, to dinner
and anything else that Max might ask, Jane withdrew
her hand firmly. 'Thanks a lot, but no.' She smiled to
soften her refusal. 'I'm hot and scruffy and, saving your
presence, frankly done-in after a busy day. So some other
time, perhaps.'

'Of course.' Max stepped back at once. 'I tend to forget
what a slave-driver I can be. I'm not surprised that
you've had enough of my company for one day.'

Jane eyed him warily. Max looked slightly less formidable than usual, probably because his hair was
untidy, and he'd discarded his jacket and tie. But the
dark face was uncommunicative, the bright, green-
flecked eyes as fathomless as ever, making it hard to
know if he felt rebuffed by her refusal or was merely
indifferent to it, as she suspected he meant her to believe.

'You're away on Monday, of course,' she said, taking
refuge in business matters to cover the awkward moment.
'But you won't forget that there's a meeting with the
representatives of the council planning department on
Wednesday at ten?'

'I'll be back Tuesday night without fail,' he said, resigned. 'In the meantime I'll be either at the London
office or my place, if you need me. By the way,' he added
casually, 'could you send out some invitations, Jane? I
think it's time that I had this house-warming party I've
been threatening. Buffet supper for about fifty—Liz and
Jim will see to the food and drink side of it. I'll leave a
guest-list on your desk for Monday.'

As Jane said goodnight, Max stayed her by holding her wrist between his thumb and forefinger.

'Jane?' he said, looking hard into her questioning eyes.

'Yes?' she prompted.

'Are we friends again?'

'I thought we had been for some time,' she said, looking away and trying to withdraw her hand, but the long, supple fingers retained their grasp.

'Since our little argument over the Brownlows I've sensed a definite withdrawal on your part, Jane. I'd like to think our relationship capable of surviving something so irrelevant to it, you know.'

His eyes drew Jane's to his like a magnet, and they stood looking at each other steadily for a moment or two, then she nodded slowly. 'I'd like to think so too, Max. Goodnight.'

Jane was very abstracted as she walked home, and not a little regretful that she'd refused the offer of dinner. Her reasons for doing so had been so petty that Max had probably thought she was making excuses, instead of stating the literal truth that she felt grubby and untidy. For some reason Jane felt it necessary to look her best at all times when in company with Max Brigstock. There was something about him which demanded perfection, and to face him across a dinner table knowing that her blouse was crumpled and her hair in need of its daily shampoo was something that Jane was not prepared to do. So now, she thought with irony, for reasons of pure vanity she was going home to a solitary sandwich, and Max was probably off on his usual cycle ride after *his* equally solitary dinner.

Jane not only felt disturbed by Max's parting remarks, but also by his earlier comment on her lack of social life, which had struck home. Feeling that it was distinctly unwise to let herself moon over Max Brigstock she decided to do something sensible about it, and set off for London next day. She spent the night with her friend Erica, who promptly invited other friends around for a drink, which turned into the type of impromptu party Jane had enjoyed so often in the past. This time, for no reason she could think of, she felt bored.

'Had a good time, darling?' asked Olivia Calvert the following evening when Jane went home.

'Very nice,' said Jane briefly, and changed the subject by asking after the progress of the old barn at the end of Glebe Lane. It was, she was told, fast becoming an almost new barn, with a great north light let in the roof.

'When it's finished,' said Mrs Calvert, 'your father wants to paint your portrait, Jane.'

Jane groaned. 'Not again, Dad! There are two in existence already.'

'Jane at six and Jane at sixteen,' agreed her father. 'Now I've a fancy to paint Jane at twenty-six, in full flower, as you might say.' He pulled her on his knee and gave her a kiss. 'There's a look about you these days that I'd like to capture on canvas.'

'Reluctance, you mean!'

'Not a bit of it. Rather a sort of luminous expectancy, as though you were waiting for something to happen.'

'You've been at the gin!' Jane said rudely, and went off to enjoy her long-awaited bath.

CHAPTER EIGHT

THE guest-list for the forthcoming party surprised Jane when she studied it next morning. Max had invited a cross-section of Wyndcombe society which promised to be a very interesting mix. Apart from her own parents and the Whiteheads, there were the people who ran the village shop, the proprietors of the inn on the outskirts of the village, the rector and his sister, a couple of retired military gentlemen and their spouses, some farmers, and several of the people involved in the Pipers Flats development. Conspicuous by their absence were any names from the old families George Calvert called the Wyndcombe aristocracy.

No London friends either, thought Jane. This was to be a very local triumph. On her desk with the list lay a pile of engraved invitations that Max had obviously ordered in London, with blanks for Jane to fill in the names. The party had been in Max's mind for some time, she realised, rather nettled that he hadn't told her about it sooner as she wondered what the recipients would make of the invitations to 'An informal buffet supper at Phoenix House'.

After two weeks of solid rain, the previous few days had been hot and fine. London, over the weekend, had been particularly trying for Jane, who found that she had less enthusiasm for city pavements and crowds of people than of old. She was heartily glad to be back in Wyndcombe, even though her day's work at Phoenix House was a full one. Despite Max's absence she was kept busy all day, not only with the miniature mountain

113

of letters that Max had left her, but also with the constantly ringing telephone. When it was time to go home Jane was more than usually tired, both from press of work and the heat. She decided that she'd had enough. The less urgent things could wait until the following day.

'You look done-in,' observed Mrs Calvert after the dinner she and Jane ate alone. George Calvert was temporarily in London again, working on a portrait commissioned by a famous legal lion.

'Busy day,' said Jane who, tired though she was, felt restless once the meal was cleared away.

'Do you enjoy working on your own when Max is away, darling?'

'Yes. It's challenging.'

'And exhausting, by the look of you. Why don't you have an early night?'

Jane hovered at the open windows, watching the stars appear one by one in the darkening sky. 'I don't really feel like sleep.' She gave her mother a sudden, mischievous smile. 'What I really fancy is a swim.'

'Go and have one, then,' said Mrs Calvert placidly. 'Max won't mind if you make use of that famous pool of his while he's away. I'm sure.'

Jane needed no second bidding. She ran upstairs to change into a swimsuit, pulled a sweatshirt and jeans over it, then ran down to collect her car keys, and kissed her mother goodbye.

Ten minutes later Jane was letting herself into the blissfully cool water of the pool hidden behind the walls of the sunken garden at Phoenix House. Max had installed lights among the trees for his regular late-night swims, and Jane watched insects fluttering against the glowing discs as she back-stroked languidly through the water, revelling in the cool caress of water gliding against her skin. After a while she turned over and completed several lengths of the pool, in the stylish, speedy crawl learned at school, then as she flipped over on her back again she opened her mouth to scream, swallowed water and sank below the surface before rising, spluttering, her eyes like saucers on the tall figure outlined against one of the lights.

'Jane?' said Max's familiar voice, and she almost went under again in her relief.

'You startled me,' she said, coughing, and swam over to the side. Max reached down a hand to help her up, hauling her effortlessly out of the water to stand dripping beside him. Jane tossed her wet hair back, feeling guilty and embarrassed, and ridiculously shy. 'I hope you don't mind—I didn't expect you back tonight—not that I've ever swum here before when you were away,' she added, floundering absurdly, conscious that Max was looking at her as though he'd never seen her before. Which he hadn't the way she looked now, she realised, looking about her hastily for the towel that she'd flung on the grass. Her swimsuit was a reasonably respectable black one-piece affair, but it nevertheless exposed more of her to her companion than he'd ever been privileged to see before.

'Is this what you want?' asked Max, spotting the towel. He handed it to her, his face hidden in the shadows as she almost snatched the towel from him in her embarrassment.

'Thanks.' Jane enveloped herself in it, shivering a little.

'You're cold.' Max rubbed his hands briskly over her towelling-covered shoulders. 'You need to get your circulation going——'

Abruptly he was silent. His hands halted in their task, his fingers suddenly biting into her shoulders as his eyes stared down into hers, first startled, then burningly intent by the soft light from the lamps.

'And this,' he said, in a voice husky with revelation, 'is what *I* need,' And he pulled her against him and kissed her so thoroughly, and with such uninhibited pleasure, that Jane was taken completely by surprise.

The towel fell to the ground, unnoticed by either of them. Jane's shivering increased at the touch of Max's fingers on her bare skin. His hands moved over her back with mounting insistence, moulding her against his body, which felt hard and urgently male, and which was an excitingly exact fit against her own. Mixed in with shock and heat, and other sensations Jane was in no fit state to categorise, was an intense feeling of recognition. Her mouth opened in astonishment and Max gave a smothered, helpless sort of groan which surprised her even more. Coherent thought ceased abruptly as his mouth crushed hers, his arms tightened convulsively, and a powerful wave of need engulfed them both like a tidal wave. Max's fingers tugged impatiently at the swimsuit while his mouth slid down her throat to her breasts, his lips seeking the hard tips, which sprang free, erect with cold and excitement, and Jane gasped, her head flung back in total abandon.

A blinding flash of lightning intervened like an act of God. It turned night to day for an instant, followed immediately by a great crack of thunder which seemed to split the heavens in two, and Jane wrenched herself out of Max's arms with a scream of pure terror, forgetting that she was half naked. Max swore with bitter fluency as he rescued the towel and draped Jane in it with ungentle hands.

'My clothes——' she gasped through chattering teeth, then screeched again as the garden lights went out.

'Hell and damnation!' Max searched frantically in his pockets for a lighter, which proved unnecessary as a second blaze of lightning provided all the illumination anyone could need. Max snatched up the bundle he found on the grass, grabbed Jane by the hand and dragged her with him as he made for the house. He had no need to urge her along. Another deafening crack of thunder lent such speed to her flying feet that she was before him as they reached the open windows of the morning-room. Max bundled her inside, slammed the windows shut, thrust her clothes into her hands and ordered her to stay where she was in the dark while he went off to find a torch.

The primitive dread that Jane experienced in thunderstorms battled for supremacy with several other clamorous emotions as she tugged the sweatshirt and jeans over her damp swimsuit, reluctant to get rid of the latter in the darkness for lack of somewhere to put it. The next peal of thunder was farther away and Jane calmed down slightly, no longer cold. In fact, she found, as she towelled her hair, she was burning with embarrassment. What in heaven's name had possessed Max to make love to her like that out of the blue? And, more important still, what had she been thinking of to let him? Not only to let him, but to respond with such out and out abandon that Jane shuddered to think what might have happened if the storm hadn't intervened so dramatically at that precise moment.

Now that the storm was receding Jane wondered if it was worth trying to slip away, to make a run for it to her car to escape facing Max. Then the lights came on and she blinked, dazzled, and Max appeared in the open doorway—it was too late.

'It was just the trip-switch, not a power-cut, fortunately,' he announced, so businesslike that Jane wondered for a wild moment if she'd imagined the scene by the pool.

'Oh, good,' she responded inanely, and busied herself with folding the towel she'd been clutching in front of her like a shield.

'Why don't you go up to one of the bathrooms and dry yourself properly,' suggested Max. 'I'll have made some coffee by the time you get back.'

'Oh, no—no.' Jane took an involuntary step backwards towards the windows. 'I really must go—my mother will be frantic—she knows how frightened I am by storms.'

'So do I—now!' he said, with such bitter emphasis that Jane flushed scarlet. 'In which case it might be as well if you wait until the storm is over before you attempt to drive home. I'll ring your mother in the meantime.'

Despite an overwhelming desire to escape, Jane did as he said, going upstairs to the bathroom where she had taken to keeping a few of her own things. Consequently her outer appearance was soon restored to some semblance of normality, which had nothing to do with how she felt inside. Somehow or other, she knew, she had to go back down there and drink coffee and try to put her relationship with Max Brigstock back on an even keel. Jane squared her shoulders, wriggling a little at the discomfort of the damp suit beneath her sweatshirt, and marched back downstairs.

Max was waiting for her in the hall. His shirt, she noticed with a clench of stomach muscles, had a large damp patch on the front, and his thick black hair was still wildly untidy from its treatment at her clutching hands in those last few frenzied moments before the storm broke.

'I rang your mother and told her that you were waiting until the storm passed. Let's go in the kitchen,' he added. 'It's warmer in there.'

Jane felt horribly awkward as she sat at the table in the middle of the large, immaculate kitchen, where Max had switched on the oil-fired Aga while she was upstairs. He poured strong black coffee into two tall mugs and added sugar without consulting her.

'I've put some brandy in it,' he warned, and sat down facing her across the table.

Jane sipped gratefully, feeling a little better as the warmth of the spirit began to permeate through her. Her teeth caught in her lower lip as she wondered uneasily if steam was likely to rise from her damp swimsuit once her body heat began drying it out.

'Daisy gave me this as a pick-me-up on the night of the fire,' she remarked inconsequentially, when she could stand the silence no longer.

'Disaster certainly tends to dog your footsteps,' Max said, with an irony which stung Jane into reminding him of his own presence at both the disasters he had in mind.

'Ah, but you can add a cancelled wedding to your score!' he reminded her swiftly.

Jane glared across the table at him, and Max sighed.

'I'm sorry, Jane. We're both snapping at each other for very obvious reasons. Speaking for myself, at least, I haven't recovered from the episode at the pool.'

Jane's colour rose again. 'Please——'

Max held up a hand, a sardonic glint in his eyes. 'I know you're so embarrassed you can't look me in the face, Jane. Nevertheless, if we don't refer to it in some way it's going to be difficult to work together in future.'

Jane took in a deep breath, then swallowed the last of her coffee. 'It was—was just one of those things,' she muttered. 'Nothing to make a fuss about. Let's just forget it. Go on as though nothing had happened.'

He raked a hand through his dishevelled hair. 'All right. I'll do my best. To go on as though it had never happened, I mean. But I can't promise to forget about it. I have a nasty feeling that I'll lie awake at night all too often, wondering just what might have happened if the storm hadn't broken at that particular moment.'

'Nothing very much, I don't suppose,' said Jane briskly, getting to her feet. 'It was probably just the— the surprise. Neither of us expected to see the other and, well, it just happened.'

'*What* happened?' enquired Max affably, jumping up to block her way as she moved towards the door.

Jane eyed him angrily. 'A perfectly ordinary kiss! No novelty to either of us, I'm sure. So let's drop the subject.'

Max wasn't paying attention. His eyes had fallen to the conspicuous damp patches across her breasts. He looked up at her, frowning.

'Don't tell me you put your clothes on top of that wet suit, for Pete's sake!'

'Yes, I did,' she snapped. 'So if you don't mind, I'm going home to have a hot bath.'

'You can have one here.'

'I want to go home!'

They stood looking at each other in an atmosphere charged with sudden tension. Max rubbed his chin, his eyes half-veiled by enviably thick lashes.

'Can you really describe what happened out there as— how did you put it?—"a perfectly ordinary kiss"?'

Jane backed away. 'Yes,' she said breathlessly, annoyed to find that she couldn't tear her eyes away from his.

'Would you consent to a little experiment?'

She swallowed. 'What sort of experiment?'

Max moved nearer. 'I'm deeply curious. I'd like to prove for myself the accuracy of your description regarding this perfectly ordinary kiss. *Then* I'll let you go home.'

To Jane, in her present overwrought state, Max looked for all the world like a tiger about to pounce. She ran the tip of her tongue over dry lips as her eyes measured the distance to the door.

Max chuckled softly.

'The price of escape, Miss Jane Calvert. One kiss, freely given.'

'Freely given!' she retorted. 'You ask a lot.'

'And usually receive it,' he informed her, then covered the space between them so quickly that his mouth was on hers before she had time to protest.

But this time Jane was forewarned enough to stand stiff and unyielding in his embrace, by some super-human effort damping down the hot gush of response which leapt inside her at the touch of his lips.

After a moment Max raised his head and stepped back.

'You were right after all,' he said casually. 'I have, as you said, experienced a fair few kisses in my time—but not one of them was more ordinary than that!'

Not for the first time Jane found it difficult to turn up for work at Phoenix House next day, and in this instance felt infinitely more reluctant than after the quarrel over the landscape gardeners. Max was in his study before her, looking irritatingly rested and fit as she went past on her way to her own sanctum. He was dressed, as always, with the careless elegance which was his hallmark in one of the lightweight tweed jackets he often wore in Wyndcombe, as a change from the formal suits he kept for the City. To Jane's relief he was deep in a telephone discussion with the architect of Pipers Flats, which meant that the moment of confrontation would be postponed for a while.

Her night had been anything but restful. As a result she'd taken extra pains with her appearance as a matter of pride, forced to resort to more make-up than usual to disguise the evidence of her sleepless night. In the end she'd left home for Phoenix House reasonably satisfied with her appearance: not a hair of her long shining bob out of place, her cream silk shirt and black linen suit new enough and smart enough to lend her confidence for the ordeal of meeting Max face to face.

Jane sorted the mail, then made a start on some of the work left over from the day before. She was wrestling with a stubborn bit of syntax on the screen of her word processor when she realised that she was being watched, and looked up to see Max in the doorway.

'Good morning, Jane,' he said abstractedly, feeling about in his jacket pockets. 'Can you lay hands on the feasibility studies I had from Wynd Construction—where the hell's my pen! I had it a minute ago.'

Jane relaxed. Everything was normal. Last night was last night, apparently. And today was just another day—heaven be praised. She smiled as she handed him the required report.

'Good morning,' she said briskly. 'Your pen's behind your ear.'

Within a remarkably short time Max had given her a demand for coffee, a list of people to get together for a meeting, dictated several letters, asked her opinion on the guest-list for the following week's party and provided her with enough work to get through to last her for the rest of the day, even without her backlog.

Jane was on her way out of the room to get on with it when Max called her back, eyeing her speculatively.

'I half expected your notice on my desk this morning, Jane.'

She went cold. 'You can still have it if you wish.'

'You know damn well I don't!' he shot back with un-characteristic heat. 'I was, in my peculiarly oblique way, trying to indicate that I was grateful for *not* having it.'

'Ah. I see.' Jane smiled coolly.

'Do you?' His smile was sardonic, as the telephone provided Jane with a welcome means of escape.

Otherwise the day went by marked by nothing more than the usual hustle and activity which invariably marked Max Brigstock's presence in Wyndcombe. Liz Collins, who was now in residence with her Jim at Dower Cottage, provided Jane with a tray of sandwiches and coffee at lunchtime, acting on instructions given by Max before he'd left for Pipers Flats for the rest of the day.

'Said I was to make sure you had something to eat, in case you decided to work through your lunch hour,' said Liz, smiling.

'How did he know I was likely to do that?' asked Jane, surprised.

'I told him you often do it if you're busy.' Liz wagged a reproving finger. 'Max doesn't disapprove of the work bit, of course, being the man he is, but he gave strict instructions about suitable nourishment. What do you think of the plans for the party?' she added, which gave Jane the opportunity to ask Liz's opinion of her own particular plan to do the flowers for it herself rather than employ the services of a florist.

'I'm sure I can coax the flowers and leaves and so on from old Mr Daniels,' added Jane, smiling.

'Since he's got a very soft spot for you I shouldn't think that'll be much problem,' said Liz, laughing.

'Has he really?' said Jane, surprised.

'Well, yes. You're Miss Olivia's girl to Daniels, Jane. Not an outsider like Max—and Jim and me.'

Jane was very thoughtful after the young housekeeper left. It had never occurred to her that the approval she took for granted was hers because of her family background. Yet it should have, she realised. It was the main reason why Max had employed her, after all. Finding that she cared less for the last idea than expected, Jane immersed herself in work, making a face at the thought of how much of it she still had to get through. She was far from ready to leave when Max returned several hours later.

'What the blazes are you doing here?' he barked. 'It's after six.'

'Earning my salary, boss,' she retorted, and went on with the report she was typing.

Max said something brief and excessively vulgar, then switched off her machine at the socket.

Jane watched in horror as three pages of hard work vanished from the screen.

'Oh, thank you! Thank you *very* much,' she said through her teeth. 'I hadn't committed that to the machine's memory. That's about a thousand carefully edited words straight down the drain!'

For once Max looked completely discomfited. 'Hell—Jane, I'm sorry. I didn't think.' He thrust a hand through his hair. 'I've come straight from a set-to with one of the builders; one of the brickies on site broke a leg today, and somehow it seemed the last straw to get home to find you still slaving away at this time of night.'

Jane extracted the disk from the machine with dangerous care, hanging on to her self-control with every last shred of strength she could muster as she slotted it into its envelope, then locked it away in the dust-proof metal box she used for storage.

'Goodnight,' she forced herself to say, as she collected her jacket.

Max sprang forward to help her into it, but Jane dodged away, and his face darkened ominously.

'Don't worry,' he snarled, 'I'm not about to lay my ill-bred hands on you again—and just to keep you happy I'll pay extra money for the time necessary to retype the bloody report.'

'Money,' Jane flung at him disdainfully, 'isn't everything.'

His eyes narrowed to a scathing glitter. 'I seem to have heard that somewhere before. Your needle's stuck, Miss Calvert.'

They stood glaring at each other for a moment, then Max sighed heavily, the tension draining from his face.

Jane felt her own anger subside in response, and her shoulders slumped. 'I'm sorry,' she said wearily. 'I don't know why I made such a fuss. It won't take long to redo the report in the morning. It must be this heat. I hope to heaven that it doesn't thunder again tonight.'

Max rubbed his chin ruefully. 'I wish it hadn't thundered last night!'

Jane's eyes flew to his, read the unmistakable meaning glinting in them and coloured to the roots of her hair.

'I thought we agreed to forget that last night ever happened,' she muttered, her eyes falling.

'So far I'm not having much success.'

'I must go,' said Jane quickly, and made for the door into the hall, but Max caught her hand.

'Stay and have a drink with me. Please!' he added, such a deep, cajoling note in his voice that Jane's knees trembled. She shook her head.

'No. I'm late already. My parents will be waiting.'

But before she could reach the door Max was before her, his shoulders planted square against the oak panels. Jane's protest was stifled at source as he pulled her to him, kissing her until she was silenced, as much by her own response as by the lips demanding, and receiving it. To her amazement she yielded to him without a struggle, utterly powerless to resist, something she'd never experienced in her life before; and Max took full advantage of it, holding her so close that she was left in no doubt of his body's response.

Several revelatory minutes passed before Jane found the strength from somewhere to tear herself away. She smoothed her hair away from her hot face, struggling to breathe normally. Max remained where he was, arms folded, still and rigid-faced as always. Except for his breathing, which was as ragged as hers, Jane would have thought him quite unaffected by the exchange.

'This is an impossible situation,' she said after a while, when she could trust her voice. 'I've never suffered this type of treatment before from an employer——'

'Suffered?' he queried silkenly.

Jane's chin rose. '"Experienced", then, if you prefer. Whatever one chooses to call it, this sort of thing just isn't possible in a viable working relationship.'

He eyed her thoughtfully for a while, then gave a rueful shrug. 'I suppose that means I must promise not to attempt anything similar again—until you request it, perhaps.'

'That'll be the day!'

'One I await with anticipation,' Max informed her, with a very unsettling gleam in his eyes. 'In the meantime, unless you give me an indication that my attentions are welcome, Miss Jane Calvert, I shan't inflict them on you in future, in working hours or out. I'll admit I let my instincts rule just then for a moment. I'm sorry. Nevertheless, I was wildly curious to prove something.'

Jane's eyes narrowed. 'What, exactly?'

'Whether the—er—rapport I fancy is growing between us rather rapidly was a figment of my imagination. And it isn't, is it?' One of Max's straight eyebrows rose lazily. 'However much you dislike the idea, Jane, there's no getting away from the fact that you and I are highly compatible.'

'Only in a purely physical context! Otherwise, we have very little in common.' She sighed, eyeing him uneasily. 'Perhaps it might be as well if I leave after all.'

'Nonsense.' Max moved away from the door. 'You say you like the work; I'm unlikely to find a replacement easily—certainly not one so adept at dealing with people, nor one who could give me such satisfaction to employ. So why spoil a mutually convenient arrangement?'

'You were the one doing that!'

'But I won't again—unless you indicate that I may. You have my word. Besides, I think you and I make a terrific team, Jane. In our working capacity, of course! It seems a pity to spoil it.' Max smiled at her suddenly, with the warmth he displayed so seldom that Jane was never prepared for the sheer charm of it.

'It does, indeed. I'll say goodnight, then,' she said colourlessly. 'I'll see you in the morning.'

Contrary to Jane's expectations life proceeded smoothly enough in the days which followed, both at Phoenix House, where Max behaved as though nothing out of the ordinary had ever occurred, and at home, where George Calvert was in buoyant mood after completing the legal luminary's portrait to much acclaim from the sitter. Any time Jane could be persuaded to spare him was spent in Glebe Barn, working on the new portrait.

At first she'd been reluctant, pleading fatigue, boredom, reluctance to stay indoors when the weather was fine ... any excuse she could think of to avoid sitting perfectly still for long periods at a time. Eventually she came to a compromise with her father. He could paint her on condition that the pose was a natural, comfortable one, that she could read a book while he worked, and also that no longer than one hour was to be spent on each sitting. George Calvert acquiesced with surprising meekness, and subsequently Jane spent most of the following weekend attired either in a strapless evening dress of amber silk which left her shoulders bare, or in sun-top and shorts in a deck-chair outside the barn when her father allowed her to escape for a rest.

'That's a rather spectacular tan,' commented Max when he saw Jane the following Monday.

She explained about the alternate sessions of sun-bathing and posing. 'Other parents have photographs of their children—mine have portraits! And in this one Dad's aiming for a sort of gilded look, hence the tan.'

Max was intrigued. 'What happens to the portraits? Does your father sell them?'

'No fear. Mind you, he did part with the adult one of Phillida when she got married—probably as a prize to Alastair for succeeding where all men had failed before,' added Jane with a grin.

Max's eyebrows rose. 'In what way?'

Jane explained about the trail of rejected bridegrooms in Phillida's wake before Alastair Rintoul, and Max whistled.

'It must have taken a fair bit of pluck then, I imagine, for you to follow in her footsteps.'

Jane looked up quickly from the mail she was sorting. 'How nice of you to think so. I thought you'd consider it a sort of hereditary disorder. In the genes, so to speak.'

'Not now that I know you better.' Max leaned back in his chair, looking at her intently. 'As far as Dr Fry's concerned, I think you did exactly the right thing.'

'So do I,' said Jane very quietly. 'Which didn't make it any easier at the time. I wish there'd been some other way to do it—without hurting Adrian, I mean.'

'Yes. I understand.' Max gave her one of his rare, sympathetic smiles. 'Let's talk of happier things. Are all the acceptances in for our soirée?'

Jane nodded, conscious of a secret little glow of pleasure at the term 'our' in reference to the party. 'The village is agog,' she informed him. 'Those invited are having a wonderful time lording it over those who are not.' She hesitated. 'Do you mind if I ask what governed your choice?'

Max's face set in sober lines. 'It's a long story. But in brief I've invited the people who were at least civil to me in the old days.' A bleak smile played at the corners of his mouth. 'I had a paper-round then, Jane. I used to cycle from Pipers Flats at the crack of dawn, collect the papers from the village shop, distribute them to the inhabitants of Wyndcombe then cycle back to school in the town. I did odd jobs on Saturdays, too. Weeding and car-washing and so on.'

Jane stared at him incredulously. 'Then why doesn't anyone remember you? My mother says that something about you keeps eluding her, but she can never put her finger on it.'

'I never actually met your mother or the Whiteheads in those days, but there are others who knew me well enough. Not that I've actually come face to face with any of the other locals since I bought the house—at least, not with anyone who recognises me.'

'But surely your name must ring a bell?'

'There's a simple explanation for that.' Max hesitated for a moment, then shrugged. 'You may as well know the rest. In my former incarnation, as it were, I lived with my grandparents at Pipers Flats. They wouldn't have any truck with "Maxim", which was my frivolous, cinema-going mother's choice. I became Billy—my second name is William. And because I lived with my grandparents local people thought of me as Billy Jennings.' Max fell silent, gazing out of the window as though he could see pictures of his early life through the glass. Jane waited quietly, and after a while he turned back to her. 'Aren't you going to ask *why* I was dumped on my grandparents?' he asked.

'No.'

'But you're curious.'

'Very.'

'Honest lady.' Max smiled slightly. 'My father was a regular soldier who got himself killed in Suez. Shortly afterwards my mother married again, a man who didn't want me as part of the package. So I became a resident of Pipers Flats until the day I ran away to London, where I engaged in any number of pursuits it's best you don't know about. Eventually I managed to persuade an accountant to take me on and teach me the trade without the usual qualifications required.'

Jane listened in silence to the unemotional account of his childhood. It was so different from her own that she felt irrationally ashamed.

'That's a very odd look on your face,' remarked Max.

Jane grimaced. 'I was just remembering how sorry I used to feel for myself just because my parents' marriage was, well, a bit stormy at times.'

Max gave her a wry look. 'Which means, I suppose, that you feel pity for young Billy Jennings.

'Yes, I do,' said Jane candidly. 'Which is not to say that I feel any for Max Brigstock. *He's* a self-made man in the full sense of the word. Congratulations are in order for him!' She eyed him quizzically. 'So this party is a lot more than just a house-warming, isn't it?'

Max's eyes took on a metallic glitter in his dark face. 'Oh, yes, Jane. A lot more! It's my way of celebrating the return of the native, if you like. And in a style which will set every tongue wagging in a ten-mile radius, once everyone realises who I am.'

CHAPTER NINE

THE week before the party was busy. Max was called away to London towards the end of it, but was very definite in his assurances that he'd be back in plenty of time for the big day.

'I fancy you're looking forward to it with relish,' said Jane, as she checked that he had everything necessary for the trip.

'I am, I am,' he said, grinning. 'And you, Miss Calvert, are to make sure that you don't overdo things while I'm gone—you can swim to your heart's content, by the way. I promise not to frighten the life out of you this time.' He touched her cheek with a gentle finger as he took his briefcase from her, hesitated, then bent and kissed her, very gently, on the lips.

He'd done a lot more than frighten her, thought Jane, as she saw him off. Neither Adrian, nor any other man she'd ever known, had ever aroused her sexually as Max had done—and she was honest enough with herself to admit that the fact added spice to her new job, which she enjoyed far more than she'd ever anticipated; and, what was more, she missed Max when he wasn't there. Something it seemed wise to clamp down on sharply before it got out of hand. But there was no denying that her feelings were vastly changed towards him these days, for any number of reasons, not the least of which was his revelation about his childhood. Jane felt a sharp pang every time she thought of young Billy Jennings, something which coloured her entire outlook towards the spectacularly successful man he'd become.

* * *

Jane was very impressed by the choice of dishes Liz had spent all week in preparing. Max's intention had been to hire a firm of professional caterers, to save Liz so much work, but Liz wouldn't hear of it. Everything was to be prepared, or supervised, by herself, at home, with the help of the two women who came in from the village regularly to clean.

'I want people to know that this is the way Max lives,' she said to Jane. 'Anyone can hire caterers. At Phoenix House it's different.' Liz gave Jane a very straight look. 'Perhaps you could—well—mention the fact to one or two of the guests.'

Jane, who was snatching a quick cup of tea in the kitchen halfway through Friday afternoon, winked at Liz. 'Don't worry. I'll spread the word.' She perched on the corner of the big table, watching with respect as Liz transferred a whole poached salmon from a fish kettle to a serving dish with practised dexterity. 'Goodness, *I* wouldn't like to do that.'

Liz chuckled. 'And I couldn't do what you do. Especially when it comes to cozening old Daniels into stripping half the garden for your flower arrangements!'

'Talking of which, I'd better get on.' Jane slid to her feet hurriedly. 'I'm praying that everyone keeps off the phone today!'

Jane's prayers went unanswered. Friday was always the busiest day of the week, and today was no exception, party or not. As Max had instructed, anything routine was relegated to the following week, but her usual telephone liaison work gave Jane very little let-up until after five. With a sigh of relief she switched on the answering machine to deal with any further business, leaving only Max's private line in operation, then hurried off to the conservatory, where several buckets of flowers stood in line waiting for her. Jane pulled on a pair of heavy-duty rubber gloves and got to work, and before long the dining-room was fragrant with the scent of roses massed in silver bowls, to echo the rose pattern of the Limoges dinner-plates stacked ready on a side-table for the following evening.

Jane assembled delicate arrangements of carnation and fern for the tables beneath the twin Victorian mirrors, then thrust great dramatic sprays of snow-white mallow in the twin blue and white Chinese porcelain jars either side of the Scottish fireplace in the drawing-room, and was just placing the last chrysanthemum among the beech leaves in a tall copper jug in the morning-room when the phone rang in the study.

'How are things going, Jane?' asked Max. 'I'm surprised you're still there.'

'You just caught me,' she fibbed. 'Everything's well in hand—where are you, by the way?'

'In the car on the motorway. Jane—could you possibly hang on until I get there?'

'Yes, of course. Is something wrong?' added Jane.

'No. I just want to see you. Tell Liz and Jim to get off home.'

After the Collinses had left for Dower Cottage, Jane went upstairs and took a hasty shower, then went back down to wander through the flower-decked rooms, smiling with satisfaction as she pictured the effect the opulence of it all would have on the natives of Wyndcombe in twenty-four hours' time.

Jane was tired, yet far too restless to sit and watch Max's television in the morning-room, or read one of his vast collection of books. As the light began to fade she went out into the gardens to check that the loud-speakers strung earlier in the trees were placed unobtrusively, as promised. Satisfied that they were almost invisible, she went back into the house to test them with one of the compact discs from Max's impressive collection, then drifted out on the terrace again, to lean back in one of the cane chairs with eyes closed as the strains of Vivaldi stole through the air.

'Very appropriate,' said a familiar voice, and Jane shot to her feet to see Max standing a few feet away grinning at her, his jacket slung by its loop over his shoulder, his shirt glimmering palely in the dusk.

Jane stood rooted to the spot, her heart thudding at the sight of him. She managed a smile. 'It's "Summer" from the *Four Seasons*.'

'I know.' He moved nearer. 'Hello, Jane.'

'Hello.'

'Have you missed me?'

'Yes.'

He laughed. Rather breathlessly, she thought with wonder.

'I've missed you, too, Jane.' He dropped his jacket on the grass and stood very still, his eyes locked with hers, and without volition Jane answered the appeal in them, running into arms which shot out to imprison her in a crushing embrace.

'Is *this* the day?' he demanded, as she smiled up at him radiantly.

'What day?'

'The day you make that request we once discussed.'

'Oh. That day! I rather think it must be.' She caught her breath at the sudden blaze in his eyes and buried her face against his shoulder.

'I've waited with a patience very foreign to me since that night, Jane,' he said huskily into her hair. 'I just can't wait any more. I've driven here like a maniac just for this. Only this, if that's how you want it. I just needed to feel you in my arms. If you prefer I won't even kiss you——'

'Why not?' she said against his shirt, and Max laughed exultantly and tipped her face up to his, looking down at her for a long moment before he bent to kiss her mouth. Once begun he seemed unable to stop long enough even to breathe, and Jane slid her arms round his neck and stood on tiptoe to return his kisses with a passion which rocked him on his feet. Max bent and picked her up in his arms. Jane gave a squeak of surprise as he strode along the terrace with her and sat down on a cane sofa with her on his lap.

'What is it?' he asked, as he lay back, holding her close.

'Apart from my father, no man's ever carried me anywhere before,' Jane confessed, utterly ravished by the experience.

Max chuckled, his lips raising shivers as they wandered over her jaw and down her throat. 'Not even the learned doctor?'

'Bad manners,' shivered Jane, making no attempt to hide the effect he was having on her. 'Not done to discuss former partnerships at a time like this.'

'Then I won't. I apologise. Let's kiss and be friends.' He acted on his words to such effect that neither of them noticed that the music had stopped, nor how dark it had grown, nor that Jim Collins came round the corner of the house, stopped dead in his tracks and stealthily went away again.

'Is this how you behave with all your friends?' said Jane, when they separated long enough to breathe.

'No,' said Max, and fell to kissing her again, his fingers lingering on the line of her throat before descending, drawn like a magnet to the curves below, to nipples which sprang up in response to his touch. Jane gave a choked sound and shivered uncontrollably, and Max tore his mouth away, rubbing his cheek over and over against her hair. He locked both arms around her, and by mutual consent they lay very still, until at last Max sat up carefully, putting Jane a small distance away from him on the sofa.

'I don't have to tell you how much I want you, Jane,' he said unsteadily. 'If I'd followed my instincts I'd have kept on going when I picked you up, all the way upstairs to my bed.'

'How do you know I'd have let you?'

'That's the point—I didn't. Which is why we're out here on the terrace right now, and why I'm talking to you instead of making love to you, locked away from the world in my room.'

Jane's teeth chattered at the picture his words painted.

'I'd better go home,' she said, jumping up, but Max caught her hand, pulling her back down on the sofa.

'You haven't asked me why I'm late, Jane.'

'I haven't asked you anything! I assumed you got held up in the City.'

Max put out a hand to her cheek, stroking it with a tenderness so new and so seductive that Jane turned her head impulsively to touch his hand with her lips. He gave a sharp intake of breath, then slid his arms around her and kissed her very gently. He raised his head and looked down into her rapt face.

'There was something I had to do first—before I came home to you.'

'Is it necessary for me to know what it was?'

'No. But I'll tell you if you wish.'

Jane smiled, and shook her head. 'You don't have to.' She jumped to her feet, holding out her hand. 'Instead, come and see what you think of the house. It's more or less ready for tomorrow.'

Max rose to his feet to take her hand, crushing it a little in his grip as he walked with her through the house, switching on lights in the immaculate rooms as they went.

'It's perfect,' he said quietly as they came to the morning-room. He looked at the flowers in the fire-place. 'Why did you insist on arranging the flowers yourself, Jane?'

'Don't you think I'm good at it?'

Max's eyes met hers, the sudden flame in them making her tremble. 'Yes, I do. But then, you're good at most things, Miss Calvert. And you didn't answer my question,' he added.

Jane chose her words with care. 'Liz insisted on doing the catering because she wanted people to know that the food was cooked here in your kitchen by your people. So I thought it would be a shame to have stiff, pro-fessional floral arrangements done by some stranger. I wanted flowers straight from your garden, arranged with loving care by your...' She halted, flushing, not sure how to go on.

'You stopped at the interesting part,' said Max softly, his eyes locked with hers. 'My what, Jane? How *would* you describe yourself?'

'Your assistant?'

He shook his head decisively. 'Not the word I have in mind. But because my self-control is a fraction pre-carious at this moment in time, it might be wise if we went on with this particular discussion tomorrow night, after the other guests have gone. Because you look a little tired, my lovely Jane.'

'You mean I look like a hag!' she joked, to disguise sudden shyness in the company of this new, beguiling Max.

'Stop fishing!' He slid an arm about her waist to walk her to the car, laying down the law about a good night's sleep, a lie-in the following morning and a lazy day before joining him a good hour before the appointed time of the party. 'I want a quiet drink alone with you before the captains and the kings arrive,' he ordered, and kissed Jane again possessively, in a manner intended to demonstrate that this was how things were to be between them from now on.

Jane drove home elated, her heart singing as she speculated on just what it was Max intended to say to her after the party. Did he mean he wanted a relationship more intimate than employer and assistant? Because he couldn't possibly have marriage in mind—could he? And if he did, what were her own feelings on the subject?

For once Jane was glad to find her parents out. She scribbled a note to leave for them when they returned from their evening stroll, and drifted in a dream up the steep flights of stairs to her new attic retreat, to lie very still on the bed, staring through the window at the stars as she relived the moments in Max's arms, wondering even now if she had imagined them. The feeling of unreality persisted as Jane remembered the bitter rancour she'd once felt for Max Brigstock, how her hackles had risen at the merest mention of his name. Whereas now… She shivered and turned over, clutching her pillow. What exactly *was* it that she felt for him now? As a man she respected him, admired him, had even forgiven him his accusation of arson. After their inopportune beginning it seemed incredible that she could have come to care so deeply for him—and without realising exactly how much until tonight, what was more. Because it wasn't Max's lovemaking which had wrought the change in her, but the new, tender possessiveness of his attitude, the gratifying knowledge that he'd driven from London at breakneck speed not only to be with her, but to make it very plain that a new stage in their relationship was about to begin.

'You never told me you owned something like that,' said George Calvert accusingly, when Jane presented herself for inspection the following evening. 'Otherwise I'd have painted your portrait in it.'

'It' was a gold silk chiffon harem-style blouse, with long, narrow sleeves and a deep, pointed neckline, worn with a skirt consisting of three layers of sand-coloured chiffon swathed about Jane's long legs sarong-style, both garments a far cry from her usual choice of clothes.

'Do you think it's a bit frivolous?' Jane asked, eyeing herself in the hall mirror. 'It's one of the outfits I bought for America—though where I ever imagined I'd wear it I don't know.'

'You look quite dazzling, Jane,' commented Olivia Calvert. 'Must be all the sunbathing.'

'Probably.' Jane spun round to face her parents. 'Are these earrings a bit over the top, do you think?'

Olivia Calvert eyed the gold filigree tassels in her daughter's ears, the glossy, sun-streaked hair, the wide eyes glittering with anticipation and something else which her feminine intuition homed in on with slight trepidation. 'You look perfect—now go on, or you won't be early as Max wanted. We'll see you later, after we've picked up Ben and Daisy.'

Jane needed no second bidding. She kissed them both and ran for her car, careless of her high fragile heels as she drove the distance to Phoenix House at a rate which made it fortunate that the narrow road which led there was deserted. She parked the car in the old coach house alongside Max's Aston Martin, then hurried into the house by way of the kitchen, where her appearance elicited loud approval from everyone present.

'Everything under control?' asked Jane, and received a chorus of good-natured assent.

'Max is in the study,' said Liz, eyes twinkling, and Jane gave her a swift kiss on the cheek and went off to find him.

Max was standing by the open french window, glass in hand, gazing out over the perfection of the gardens in the evening light. Jane was pierced by a thrust of pure possessiveness as she watched him, unseen, her eyes proprietary as they roved over the tall figure dressed in a suit of darkest charcoal grey. Against his tanned face his shirt gleamed snow-white, his silk tie a dull gold, only a few shades lighter than the eyes he turned on Jane as she stood poised at the door. A slight draught fluttered the chiffon of her skirt and she smiled, her eyes incandescent in response to the sudden leap of light in his.

'Monarch of all you survey?' she asked huskily, and moved towards him.

Max sprang to meet her halfway across the room, and took her in his arms. 'My darling, I'd like to think so,' he muttered, and kissed her with utter disregard for her appearance.

Jane kissed him back, as careless as he of something as unimportant as smudged lipstick or ruffled hair, far more occupied with the heart-stopping welcome she'd been dreaming of all day.

It was some time before Max held her away, breathing unevenly as he ran his eyes over her. 'Scheherazade, no less! Jane, you look so beautiful, I'm not sure I'll let you come to the party.'

Jane's eyes gleamed artlessly. 'After all the effort I've made? Why not?'

Max grinned, and ran a fingertip over her bottom lip. 'Because, my darling, even though I know I can't, I fancy

I can see through that flimsy stuff you're wearing, which means that every other man will feel the same and I'll want to black their wandering eyes.'

'I'm perfectly respectable!' she protested, her face hot. 'I'm wearing a silk camisole, and the skirt is lined.' She glanced down at herself, frowning. 'I did wonder if it was a bit much, but my parents thought I looked all right.'

Max laughed a little unsteadily, and held her close. 'Oh, you do, you do, Miss Calvert. So much so that I yearn to carry you off to somewhere quiet and private right now, to take up where we left off last night.' He kissed her again, slowly, with mounting fervour, and Jane trembled and slid her arms round his neck, returning his kisses with rapture for a few electric moments before gently pushing him away.

'Now look at me!' she said with mock severity, as she smoothed back her hair.

Max smiled, his eyes lingering on the low neckline. 'I am looking!'

'It took ages to get myself ready, and you've demolished all my good work in a few moments, Mr Brigstock.'

'Ah, but what moments they were!' Max moved nearer with an intent gleam in his eye, and Jane retreated, laughing.

'Oh no, you don't. I'm going upstairs to make some repairs, then I'll come back down for a drink.'

Max reached out a hand to touch her glowing cheek. 'Don't be long. I promise to behave—for the moment, anyway.'

He was as good as his word. When Jane returned, groomed and shining once more, Max took her into the dining-room to see the display achieved by Liz and all her helpers. Jane had seen quite a number of the dishes in preparation, but her eyes widened incredulously as she viewed the finished array of food laid out for the delectation of Max's first guests at Phoenix House.

'A bit ostentatious, do you think?' asked Max, sliding an arm round her waist. 'Just a touch of the vulgar?'

Jane leaned against him involuntarily, not even aware that she was doing so, and Max's arm tightened, his eyes on her face as she examined the remarkable range of dishes Liz had achieved.

It was a banquet fit for a king, with something like a king's ransom spent on it, Jane knew. There were half-lobsters served on the shell, king prawns and fresh dressed crab, two whole salmon on beds of greenery and nasturtium blossoms, and cold roast meats of every description, from conventional turkey to haunch of venison and breast of guinea fowl. Later the cold dishes would be joined by the hot raised game pies which Liz considered her particular specialty; also a great silver bowl of Beluga caviare. And waiting in the refrigerators in the larder, Jane knew, were puddings and confections of every description.

'It's magnificent,' said Jane in awe. She grinned up at Max. 'Liz wants me to let it be known, very casually of course, that this is how you eat every day.'

Max shook with laughter against her. 'Good lord, if I did I'd never get *on* my famous bike, let alone pedal five miles on it most nights.' He led her over to a side-table massed in readiness with serried ranks of frosted bottles. 'Right, Miss Calvert. Let me pour you some of this.'

'What is it?' asked Jane, eyeing the foaming liquid in her glass.

'Pink champagne, of course, madam—the only thing on offer tonight, apart from a rather good single malt for those males—like your father—who regard champagne as effete.' Max grinned at her audaciously.

Jane raised her glass to him, smiling as she shook her head. 'A toast, sir, to your ostentation. And,' she added, looking him in the eye, 'another to Billy Jennings.'

Max's eyes softened, and he raised his glass to her. 'My toast, my beautiful Jane, is to us!'

'To us,' she echoed, her eyes locked with his, and as they touched glasses there was an aura of commitment about the moment, as though a question had been asked, and answered, by both of them as they drained their glasses and put them down. In silence Max took Jane into his arms and held her close, careful now not to disarrange her, then, at the sound of a car arriving, he released her with reluctance, his hand gripping hers hard for a moment.

'Overture and beginners, please,' he said huskily. 'Time for the performance.'

Max insisted that Jane stood with him to receive his guests, and, as she smiled and shook hands and watched Max do the same, she realised that 'performance' was exactly the word. Max Brigstock was putting on a show for the inhabitants of Wyndcombe. Tonight he was the perfect host, hospitable and urbane as he smiled his contained, public smile and shook hands and responded to the greetings of people not only curious to meet him, but to inspect the wonders he had wrought with the house.

'I can't speak for anyone else,' said Olivia Calvert, drawing her daughter aside later, 'but *I'm* impressed. But then,' she added drily, 'I think we were all meant to be, were we not?'

Jane chuckled. 'Percipient parent! That was Max's intention, certainly.'

'And very successful, too,' said her father, eyeing his surroundings. 'Did Max choose *all* this stuff himself?'

'No. Most of it was done professionally.'

'Glad to hear it. That fireplace has a shade too much attack for this room, wouldn't you say, Olivia?'

His wife smiled as she examined it. 'Rather like its owner, I suppose.'

As Jane went off to circulate among the guests she kept her ears open, trying to catch any speculation about Max Brigstock's identity, but on the surface everyone seemed more engrossed in the splendour and cost of their surroundings. Then the Johnsons arrived, breathless and late after a busy Saturday in the village stores.

Max strode forward, hand outstretched, smiling at the elderly pair. 'Good evening; so glad you could make it. I'm Max Brigstock.'

Vera Johnson took his hand. 'Sorry we're a bit behind, Mr Brigstock. I'm so pleased to meet you.' She held on to his hand, peering up into his face. 'But—haven't we met before?'

Her husband shook his head slowly, his eyes on Max's wry, smiling face. 'Well, well, bless my soul! Am I imagining things? It's—it's young Billy, isn't it? You used to stack shelves for me on a Saturday morning.'

Mrs Johnson's jaw dropped, her eyes almost popping. *'Billy?'* she said, with a little shriek which drew all heads in her direction. 'It can't be!'

'It is,' Max assured her, mouth twitching. 'Only I go by my real name these days, Mrs Johnson, instead of my grandfather's.'

The news flashed through the assembled guests like a forest fire. The noise level soared as people exclaimed and jostled for a place near Max so that they could congratulate him and welcome him all over again, and he stood in the midst of it, a rock buffeted by waves of excitement.

'You knew?' asked Mrs Calvert, as Jane watched, tense, ready to make her way to Max if he needed her.

'Yes.'

'And you didn't say?' exclaimed Daisy Whitehead, saucer-eyed.

George Calvert looked scathing. 'Of course she didn't, Daisy. Not Jane's job to go blabbing about Max's private affairs, otherwise she wouldn't be working for the chap.'

Jane wasn't even listening. She was looking at Max, over the heads of the crowd. His eyes found hers for a moment, and with a word to her parents and the Whiteheads she began to thread her way through the guests, her friendly smile disguising her steely determination to get to Max's side.

'All right?' she asked quietly as she reached him, and he nodded.

'Just slip out and see if it's time to eat, would you, Jane? We need another focus of interest.'

Without a word Jane slipped away to the dining-room to find Liz placing the bowl of caviare in the place of honour, and everything in readiness.

Liz grinned. 'Feeding time for the lions? Give me a minute to escape and wheel 'em in.'

Jane skilfully diverted the stream of guests into the dining-room, where the noise level rose again at the sight of the lavish spread, but through the open double doors she could see that Max was still captive. She raised an eyebrow at her mother, who drifted unobtrusively towards Max, rescuing him from the clutches of two of the contractors' wives with a skill any diplomat would have envied.

'Well done, Liv,' muttered her husband.

'I merely followed instructions,' said Mrs Calvert, as Max heaved a sigh of relief.

'Jane?' he enquired with a grin. 'Is she all right? I ought to be there with her, making sure everything's going smoothly.'

Olivia smiled. 'Perhaps I could help with that. I'll send Jane out to you for five minutes while people are tucking in.'

'Thank you. I'd appreciate some breathing space.' Max gave her a rueful smile.

Olivia returned it with interest. 'Your grandmother had a photograph of you on her bedside table, you know, Max. That's why you looked familiar to me.'

'What's that?' said her husband sharply.

'I'll explain later, George. Come along. Time to eat.' Olivia took her husband's arm, hurrying him along into the dining-room, and a few moments later Jane made her escape to join Max.

'Are you all right?' she asked.

He seized her hand and pulled her along the hall, making for his study. He thrust her inside and pulled the door shut, leaning against it as he'd done before as he drew her into his arms.

'Why did I subject myself to all this?' he demanded roughly. 'I loathe parties.'

Jane put a hand up to his face. 'This is a special party, Max. Look on it as a tribute to your grandparents, *and* to young Billy, not just a celebration for Max Brigstock. So kiss me, please, then let's join the others. Let your hair down and do a bit of unashamed gloating!'

Max groaned, then laughed and bent to kiss her up-turned mouth. 'I like the first bit best. You promise to stay later?' he added urgently. 'Just for a while after everyone's gone?'

'Just try to send me home!' She caught his hand. 'Come on. Back to the fray.'

From then on Max kept to his role of faultless host, mixing and mingling with his guests, pressing them to more food, more drinks, chatting and smiling, circulating at regular intervals so that his attention was bestowed equally on one and all. It was some time later before he managed to make his way to Jane again.

'Have you eaten anything?' he asked in an undertone.

'No. Have you?'

'No. We'll have a little feast of our own—when everyone's gone.' He touched her hand, then looked up as Jim Collins tapped him on the shoulder.

'Sorry to intrude. Late arrival, waiting for you in the hall.'

Max exchanged a narrowed glance with Jane. 'I thought everyone was here.'

She frowned. 'So did I. We did a count before the meal.'

They made for the door swiftly, impeded now and then as people stopped them to enthuse. When they finally emerged into the hall Jane felt Max stiffen as he saw the figure standing motionless, backlit dramatically by the sunset light streaming in through the open door. The newcomer was a woman, a stranger to Jane; slim and svelte in a black crêpe jump-suit which hugged every curve of her body. Her hair gleamed like a cap of ebony in the ruby light, her black eyes glittering with triumph above her smiling, scarlet-lipped mouth.

CHAPTER TEN

MAX stood motionless, like a figure turned to stone, at the sight of his visitor. Jane's startled eyes shot from the quickly shuttered anger in his eyes to the woman, who waited there, smiling at him, and all at once Jane felt overdressed and horribly girly in her chiffon against the late arrival's stark, unornamented chic.

'Hello, Max,' said the woman in a low, husky voice which curved Jane's fingers into talons at the mere sound of it. 'Sorry I'm late. But you must have known I wouldn't miss your house-warming, darling.'

'I *should* have known,' agreed Max harshly.

The woman held out her hand to Jane. 'Since Max is in no rush to introduce me I'll do it myself. I'm Kristin Muir, and I design interiors for people with lavish tastes—like Max.'

Jane nodded coolly, touching the scarlet-tipped hand for the briefest of acknowledgements, secretly astonished that someone dressed so simply could have decorated Max's house with such opulence. 'How do you do? I'm Jane Calvert.'

'Jane is my personal assistant here at the Wyndcombe base,' said Max expressionlessly.

'How interesting,' said Kristin Muir, in a way which implied the precise opposite. Ignoring Jane, she linked her arm through Max's, smiling up at him coaxingly. 'Do introduce me to some of that congenial-sounding gathering in there, darling. I'm in just the mood to party.'

Max looked at Jane in appeal, holding out his free hand. 'Come with us.'

She smiled brilliantly. 'No, no, you take Ms Muir to mingle. I'll just see how Liz is getting along.' She turned on a slender satin heel and went off in the direction of the kitchen, but once out of sight took a swift detour up the back stairs to take refuge in one of the bedrooms for a moment or two. One look at Kristin Muir had made it clear, beyond all possible doubt, that whatever the lady's present relationship with Max might be it had once been a great deal more than mere client and designer, and Jane badly needed time to adjust to the discovery.

Jane slumped on a stool in front of the dressing-table in one of the bedrooms, eyeing her stormy reflection with distaste. The gold tassels looked oddly tawdry now. She longed to tear them from her ears, wishing passionately that she'd kept to her usual style and worn something plain and elegant and more... Jane eyed herself in derision. More like the dangerous-looking Ms Muir? She jumped up, smoothing down the intricately draped skirt; then halfway to the door she caught Max's name, and realised that she could hear snatches of conversation floating up through the open window from below as men strolled after dinner on the terrace. Jane found that she could even smell cigar smoke on the evening breeze, and went back to flatten herself behind the curtain at the window, eavesdropping shamelessly.

'Lucky blighter, this Brigstock. Young Jane to run after him down here and that man-eating creature up in London...'

Jane went hot all over. The voices receded and came back again as the men wandered back and forth below, incomplete snippets of conversation tantalising Jane at her vantage point.

'Damn striking woman—she can do me over any time...' Their raucous laughter set Jane's teeth on edge. It faded into the distance, then all was quiet. Jane took

in a deep breath, bracing herself to go back downstairs.
The arrival of Kristin Muir might have ruined it; nevertheless, the evening was by no means over. But before
Jane could move she heard Kristin Muir's voice, low-
pitched and breathless as she spoke urgently in a rapid
undertone that Jane couldn't catch. Then, clear as a bell,
the next words carried up to Jane on an up-draught.

'Do you like my outfit, Max?'

'Kristin——'

'No one's looking, darling. It's dark out here. Give
me your hand——'

'For heaven's sake!'

Jane's teeth clenched at the torment in Max's voice.

'I just thought you'd like to know that underneath
this little number I'm completely naked, darling...'

Jane could stand no more. She fled out of the room
and downstairs to the back hall, colliding with Jim
Collins on his way to the kitchen.

'Jane!' He steadied her, frowning as he felt her trembling. 'What's wrong?'

'Nothing, Jim—just in a hurry to get back to the party.
Going wonderfully well, isn't it?' Jane gave him a
blinding smile, her eyes glittering feverishly as she whirled
off to join the throng of guests in the drawing-room.

'Who,' said her mother, coming up behind her, 'is that
lady with Max?'

'That's no lady,' said Jane with a brittle little laugh.
'That's his interior decorator.'

'Which explains why she's wearing overalls,' observed
George Calvert, eyeing his daughter closely. 'You all
right, chicken?'

'Never better,' she assured him, her smile brightening
as Max brought Kristin Muir towards them. 'Have you
met Ms Muir?' she demanded of the Whiteheads and

launched into a spate of introductions, her eyes never quite meeting Max's stony gaze.

'What a clever daughter, Mrs Calvert,' purred Kristin. 'Such a nice little flair for flower arranging, and I gather she types, too.'

'Not nearly as talented as you, Miss Muir,' returned Olivia, smiling gently. 'If I hadn't seen it with my own eyes I wouldn't have believed what you've managed to do in *some* of the rooms here.'

Her husband took a large gulp of brandy, and the Whiteheads melted away hurriedly to talk to friends.

'I'm glad you approve,' said Kristin, looking narrowly from Max to Jane and back again. 'You should have seen the place before I began on it.'

'Oh, I had,' Olivia assured her in honeyed tones.

Max spoke for the first time. 'This was once Mrs Calvert's home.'

'My wife was a Verney,' added George casually, to his wife's surprise. Normally her thoroughbred origins were a bone of contention between them.

Kristin Muir smiled, cat-like, plainly revelling in the undercurrents crackling below the surface conversation, and Jane watched in silence, resenting her fiercely, refusing to look at Max, whose eyes, she knew very well, were willing her to look in his direction. The sudden shrill of the telephone came as a godsend and she darted off to answer it, before Max could make a move to do so himself.

The call was for Liz. Jane switched it through to the kitchen, then turned, resigned, as the study door closed softly behind Kristin Muir, who stood leaning against it in unconscious parody of Max earlier, as she barred Jane's escape.

'Some boring people from the village are monopolising Max for the moment, so I thought I'd take the opportunity to have a little chat with you, Joan,' she said, smiling.

'Jane.'

'Ah, yes. But not *plain* Jane. More like tuppence-coloured, in that rig-out, darling.'

Jane smiled sweetly. 'That sounds like one of my grandmother's arcane little sayings.'

A deep breath disturbed the thin black silk outlining Kristin Muir's breasts. 'Naughty, naughty, dear. Put your claws in.'

Jane shrugged. 'Perhaps you'd say what you came to say and let me get back out there. It's part of my duties to see to the guests' welfare, Ms Muir.'

'And what other "duties" do you perform for Max, I wonder?' parried the other with sarcasm.

'Oh, just flower arranging and the odd spot of typing. Don't you remember?'

'Good, good,' purred Kristin, brushing an imaginary fleck of dust from her black-clad hip. 'You keep to that, darling. Though I should start looking for another job, if I were you. Once Max and I are married you won't be needed any more.'

There was a pause.

'I didn't realise that congratulations were in order,' said Jane quietly.

'My dear girl, I didn't go to all the enormous trouble I took to decorate this house just for some other woman to live in it,' said Kristin Muir with a pitying smile. 'Why do you think Max gave me such a free hand? It was always intended for our weekend retreat, darling, once we were married.'

'I see. Well,' said Jane briskly, 'now you've got that off your chest perhaps you'll forgive me if I get back to the party. Things to do.' She walked towards the door with such purpose that the other woman stood away from

it rather hastily. 'So nice to have met you, Ms Muir. I
can't think why we haven't run across each other before.'

'I've been in New York, darling. I only got back this
week. Didn't you know? That's why Max came dashing
up to town on Thursday.' Kristin Muir smiled her wide,
scarlet smile and waved Jane before her. 'After you,
Joan. I think people are probably beginning to leave.'

She was right. The hall was thronged with people lining
up to thank Max for a wonderful evening, but when he
beckoned Jane to his side to speed the parting guests she
pretended not to see, and made a bee-line for her mother.

'I'll come home with you now, I think,' she said, suddenly at the end of her tether.

'Max thinks you're staying on after the others,' murmured Olivia, waving at the rector.

'Well, I'm not. I want out. But my car's blocked.'

Olivia Calvert viewed her daughter's disintegrating
composure with misgiving. 'All right. You can squash
in the Whiteheads' car with us—it's parked near the
conservatory door.'

'Fine. I'll slip out that way while you're being polite
to Max. Don't tell him I've gone.' A swift look in Max's
direction confirmed that Kristin had joined him at the
door to say goodnight to the departing guests, for all
the world as though she were already lady of the house,
and Jane turned on her heel, threading her way unobtrusively through the hall to the conservatory door. To
her deep relief the Whiteheads' car was waiting with
engine running and Ben ready at the wheel as the Calverts
pushed a surprised Daisy in after him and made room
for Jane, who sat tense and silent all the way home, not
hearing a word of the conversation her parents kept up
with Ben to prevent the questions Daisy was obviously
dying to ask.

At Pond House Mrs Calvert sent her daughter straight to bed, then went after her a few minutes later with a mug of rum-laced cocoa and a couple of aspirins.

'The rum is your father's idea. I'm not terribly sure how it will sit with pink champagne,' said Mrs Calvert.

'I didn't drink enough to make it a problem. Now I come to think of it I never got round to eating anything, either,' said Jane, accepting the cocoa gratefully.

'Shall I make you some toast?'

'No, thanks.' Jane tried to smile up at her mother's anxious face. 'That woman told me that they're getting married, you know.'

'Did you believe her?'

'I don't know.'

'Does it matter to you very much, Jane?'

Jane was slow to answer. 'Yes,' she admitted eventually, avoiding her mother's eyes. 'It matters more than anything in the world. I've fallen in love with the man, Mother. Hilarious, isn't it? I had such romantic notions about why he wanted me to stay behind tonight. Now all I have is a nasty suspicion that he was about to proposition me. If he *is* marrying Kristin Muir he might have had some idea about setting me up as his bit on the side down here in the country.'

'I don't believe that for one moment.' Mrs Calvert bent to kiss her daughter's hot cheek, smoothing away the tumbled, honey-coloured hair. 'I should wait to hear Max's side of it, Jane.'

'I'm afraid to.'

'Why?'

Jane gave a choked little laugh, her eyes sheened with sudden tears. 'Because I'm a coward. I don't want to find that I'm right.' Suddenly she sat bolt upright at the sound of squealing brakes as a car drew up outside, followed by swift footsteps on the gravel of the drive and a peremptory ring of the doorbell.

Olivia met her daughter's eyes and shrugged. 'Max, I imagine, has brought your car down for you, and by the sound of it your father's letting him in.'

'Tell him I've gone to bed,' said Jane frantically, and drew the quilt over her head, like an animal diving for its burrow. 'For goodness' sake, send him away!'

'I'll do my best.'

Jane lay rigid and hot under the covers after her mother had gone, praying that Max would go away and leave her in peace, but Mrs Calvert returned a minute or two later to inform her daughter that Max Brigstock wished to speak with her.

'What's more, your father thinks that it's best you come down. Otherwise Max looks set on sitting it out until you do.'

Jane glared up at her mother mutinously. 'Tell him I've gone to bed!'

Mrs Calvert sighed. 'I did. So he asked—very politely—if I'd mind getting you up again. Come down and get it over with, Jane. You can talk to Max in the sitting-room. George and I will take ourselves off to bed.'

Jane groaned but got up, nevertheless, in response to her mother's implacability. 'All right. But it won't do any good.'

She dragged a brush through her hair, scrubbed at her eyes, then zipped herself into an old yellow velour dressing-gown and trudged downstairs to the sitting-room, taking in a deep, unsteady breath before turning the porcelain knob on the door.

Max stood in the middle of the room waiting for her, his jacket thrown down on a chair. His tie was missing and his shirtcuffs turned back, as if he was ready to do battle.

'What do you want?' asked Jane, standing just inside the door.

'You know damn well what I want,' he said angrily. 'Why the hell did you run away like that?'

'I'd had enough.' Jane pushed a hand through her hair, her heavy eyes defiant. 'I resign. I won't work for you any more.'

'Why?' He stood with legs apart and arms folded across his chest, his face taut.

'I'm not in the market for fun and games with married men,' she said flatly.

'What in blazes are you drivelling about! I'm not married.'

Jane's chin lifted. 'But I have it on the best authority that you soon will be.'

'Kristin?'

'The very same.'

Max's shoulders sagged suddenly, and he rubbed a hand over his chin. 'May I sit down?'

'Of course.' Jane closed the door carefully, then went over to one of the wing chairs at the fireplace.

Max slumped down opposite her, his eyes dull as they met hers. 'The marriage bit was always Kristin's idea. Never mine.'

'But you *are* lovers.'

'Not for a long time, if you can bring yourself to believe it.'

'Kristin seems to think differently. She was very explicit on the subject.' Jane gave a wry little shrug. 'I don't know why I reacted so violently. Presumptuous, really. It isn't as though there was anything—anything concrete between you and me.'

Max's eyebrow rose in sardonic question. 'You mean you allow all your employers to make love to you?'

Jane flushed. 'We exchanged a few kisses, Max, that's all. No big deal.'

Max's look flayed her. 'A few kisses. That's all it was to you, then. I might have known. You haven't changed after all.'

'What do you mean?'

'I should have realised that the social gap between Miss Jane Calvert of Wyndcombe and Max Brigstock, one-time inhabitant of Pipers Flats, still yawns like the Grand Canyon. My money, my achievements—none of it has really changed anything from your point of view. To you I'm still an interloper, even now.' He rose to his feet slowly, looking about him as though he was seeing the room properly for the first time. 'I'm sorry I barged in here like a fool. Your parents were remarkably for-bearing. I wouldn't have blamed your father if he'd thrown me out, neck and crop.'

'Why should he do that?'

Max's smile was bleak. 'He might have doubted my intentions towards you. As you did.'

They stared at each other in silence, then Jane blurted out the question which had been burning inside her all evening. 'Why *did* you ask me to stay after the party, Max?'

He shrugged. 'Good question. My reasons seemed good enough at the time. Now they don't. I was an idiot, I suppose, to contemplate what I had in mind.' He rubbed his eyes wearily. 'I must go—apologise to your parents for me. Goodnight.'

'I—I'll come back on Monday and clear up the work I left.'

Max's eyes iced over. 'No! I'd rather you didn't. If you must go I'd rather make the break now. I'll get someone down from the London office to take over.' His eyes lingered for a moment on the tear-stains under hers, and Jane held her breath, certain for a moment that he was going to bend down, scoop her up in his arms and assure her that Kristin Muir was nothing to him, that Jane Calvert was the only woman in the world he wanted. But Max stepped back, and her eyes dropped to her clasped hands, blinking fiercely to keep back the tears.

'By the way,' he said, off-hand. 'Kristin is staying the night at Dower Cottage with Liz before she drives back tomorrow—if it's of any interest to you.'

The lump in Jane's throat kept her speechless.

'I see that it isn't.' Max gave a mirthless chuckle. 'Funny, really. The first time I ever laid eyes on you I knew you were trouble.'

Jane swallowed determinedly, and cleared her throat. 'When I knocked you off your cycle,' she said huskily.

To her surprise Max sat down again. 'No, earlier than that. I saw you for the first time eighteen or nineteen years ago.'

Jane frowned. '*I* don't remember it.'

Max's eyes lit with a cold gleam of mockery. 'Ah, but I do. It was in the grounds of Verney House one summer afternoon. I was trying to catch some forbidden fish, as usual, but the fish weren't biting and I was hot, so I stripped off and had a swim instead. When I came out of the water—minus clothes—I was set on by a small fury with blonde plaits who called me a nasty horrible trespasser and screamed at me to get off Verney land.'

Jane stared at him in astonishment. 'That was *you*?'

Max nodded. 'And very rude you were. Little Miss Calvert ran me off her patch like Wyatt Earp cleaning up the West.' His eyes challenged. '*Now* do you remember?'

Jane remembered all too well. Her cheeks grew hot at the thought of it. 'Yes,' she muttered. 'But I had no idea it was you.'

'Have I changed so much?'

Jane coloured, her eyes sliding away from his. 'I wouldn't know. The reason I behaved like the fury you mentioned was because I was only eight years old and frightened out of my wits at the apparition which suddenly materialised in front of me on the river bank. And, well, to put it politely it was the first time I'd ever seen a completely nude male.'

Max coughed a little. 'You mean you never looked at my face.'

She nodded, expecting scornful laughter. Instead Max leaned across and put a finger under her chin to raise her face to his, and she tensed, her colour receding at his touch.

'In actual fact you did me a good turn that day, Jane.'

Her smile was bitter. 'By hounding you off property that wasn't even mine?'

'That was the day I decided that no one would ever speak to me like that again in my life, that I was going to get out of Pipers Flats and make enough money to buy a place like Verney House and get my own back on that snotty little kid.' Max laughed shortly. 'When I got out of the pool that day at Phoenix House and saw you standing there on the grass I had a job to keep a straight face when I realised who you were. History repeating itself!'

'Is that why you offered me the job?' asked Jane quietly. 'To gloat over our role reversal?'

'Yes,' he said honestly. 'I won't deny it. It gave me enormous satisfaction to employ Miss Jane Calvert, to give her orders and have her fetch and carry for me. I'm only human, Jane. It was wonderful balm for the bruises my ego still had, even after all those years. But make no mistake, I'm too good a businessman to pay out money to someone not worth her salt. If that snotty little girl had turned into a snotty, brainless woman I wouldn't have given her a second thought. But she hadn't. She'd become a beautiful, warm, intelligent woman whom I found, almost against my will, fitted every requirement I'd ever harboured regarding the opposite sex. You were the exact woman I wanted for the job—a woman who not only looked and sounded like a thoroughbred, but who promised to be damned efficient on top of it. I could hardly believe my luck. And I was right. The luck ran out tonight, didn't it?'

'I assume that Kristin's appearance at the party wasn't planned?'

'Not by me.'

Jane looked at him steadily. 'I couldn't help wondering if your idea was to keep Kristin in London and me down here—in two separate compartments, so to speak. I happened to eavesdrop, quite by accident, on speculation on the subject from some of the male element at the party.'

Max jumped to his feet, his eyes glittering with distaste. 'Which not only makes your opinion of my ethics insultingly plain, but proves the old adage about eavesdroppers.'

Jane got up wearily. 'Very true. I may as well come clean and confess that I also had the misfortune to overhear Kristin telling you exactly what she was wearing—or not wearing.'

Max looked sick. 'How the hell did you manage to do that?' he demanded fiercely.

Jane explained, then looked at her watch. 'It's late. I think you should go now. Thank you for bringing my car back.'

As Max stared at her Jane saw anger blaze in his eyes fleetingly, before his usual control hardened them into the blank, metallic screens he kept between himself and the world.

He shrugged. 'Under the circumstances it's as well that I did. Now you can turn your back on Phoenix House and its owner and forget you ever had anything to do with either, can't you? Goodbye, Jane.'

'Goodbye, Max.' Her chin lifted proudly, her eyes wide and tearless as they stared into his.

He stood very still for a moment, then uttered a smothered curse and seized her in his arms, kissing her with such tormented desperation that both of them were shaking by the time he thrust her away from him at last and flung out of the room, leaving Jane in despair, feeling as though her world was in ruins about her.

CHAPTER ELEVEN

IT NEVER ceased to surprise Jane how difficult it was to come to terms with working in the City again. At one time she'd enjoyed a non-stop love-affair with London. Now, after the summer interlude in Wyndcombe with Max, she found it impossible to settle back into her former routine. Her circle of friends welcomed her back with open arms, but try as she might Jane failed to fit herself back into the life she'd once found so satisfactory and fulfilling. At first she'd occupied a cupboard-like bedroom in her father's Chelsea studio, but eventually she found a minuscule retreat of her own after securing a job in the personnel department of one of the big Oxford Street department stores.

For a while after the fateful party Jane had found it impossible to believe that she would never see Max again. Every time the phone rang or someone knocked on the door of Pond House she was sure it was Max. But at last she faced the truth. The stiff communication enclosing the money owed to her was all she was going to get. There seemed nothing to do but take herself away from Wyndcombe and all it stood for and go back to the life she'd led before she'd met him. Max, she now knew beyond all doubt, had expected her to trust him whatever Kristin might have had to say, and was not merely angry with her, but deeply hurt. Whatever it was that had begun to grow between herself and Max, Jane thought sadly, had been too delicate a plant to survive the trauma of that fateful night.

On the other hand, Jane thought irritably as the weeks passed, if it *had* been such a delicate thing, why wasn't she recovering more quickly? She'd tried hard enough. She met other men in the course of her new job, and went out with some of them, and spent time with men she'd known before Adrian, too. But the evenings rarely afforded her more than a lukewarm pleasure. After Max she had no taste for other men's kisses, and her escorts soon fell by the wayside, few of them interested in the purely cerebral form of companionship Jane had to offer.

The portrait begun in the barn at Wyndcombe was completed eventually in Chelsea. Jane was now only too pleased to sit for her father at weekends. She had nothing better to do. And these days, because Jane felt it best to keep away from Wyndcombe for a while, her mother came up to London sometimes and sat working at her tapestry during the sittings. The one great joy in Jane's life since the summer was the knowledge that her parents were back together for good. Olivia had even yielded to her husband's persuasion and allowed him to buy Pond House for her from Max, and the Chelsea studio was to be sold.

'Has your mother told you the real reason why Max offered her Pond House at such an unrealistic rent?' enquired George, as he frowned over the folds in Jane's amber silk dress.

'No.' Jane took care not to move her head from the pose, and missed the smile her parents exchanged.

'Virtue,' observed George Calvert, 'proved to be its own reward in Liv's case. She was the one who visited the old Jennings couple faithfully, every day, when they were ill, you see. Pond House was Max's anonymous way of thanking her for being kind to his grandparents. I got it out of him when we were haggling over the price.'

Jane turned appalled eyes on her father, forgetting her pose. 'Haggling! Surely you didn't try to beat him down, Dad!'

'Oh, ye of little faith! Turn your head again, child.'

'George thought the price was too *low*,' said her mother quickly. 'He thought we should have paid more.'

'Oh.'

'Max looked a bit thin when I saw him the other day,' said George casually. 'Tanned, though. Just back from Siena.'

'Home of St Catherine,' murmured Jane, her lips drooping at the thought, and her father growled and told her to keep her head still, and to stop looking so glum.

Jane, as it happened, knew first-hand that Max was thinner. About a month after her return to London she had spotted him getting out of a taxi outside Harrods and had dodged away out of sight quickly before he had had time to notice her. Afterwards she'd been furious with herself. It would have done no harm to say hello— might even have done some good. As it was it had shot her recovery programme back to square one, and she had had to start all over again.

Jane congratulated herself on doing quite well after a while. Then she came across Max again. She was having a meal with Erica in the Camden Brasserie, when Max came in with another man and was shown to a place which gave Jane a view of the back of his black, glossy head from her vantage point at the back of the long, narrow room.

'Is your steak tough?' demanded Erica.

Jane assured her that it was perfect, but was so abstracted for the rest of the meal that Erica was a trifle irritable by the time she'd paid for a meal Jane had hardly touched.

'Couldn't we hang on for a bit?' asked Jane, dreading the moment when she'd be forced to pass Max on her way out.

'Look, love, if you want more coffee come and have some at my flat. It costs less. Especially if you *leave* half of it!' added Erica pointedly, peering in Jane's cup. 'Come on. Let's go.'

Jane kept close behind her friend as they moved down the room, but Erica was a tall redhead who commanded attention wherever she went, and the man di**ning** with Max was no exception. He made an unobtrusive comment to Max, who glanced up as Erica passed, then leapt to his feet at the sight of Jane.

Jane smiled reluctantly, watched by two pairs of very interested eyes. 'Hello, Max. How are you?'

'Fine,' he said absently, his eyes running over her as if checking she was all in one piece. 'You live in Camden, Jane?'

'No. Just passing through.' Jane fidgeted, and Max recalled himself hurriedly, introducing his companion as a television producer from the TV studios nearby.

Jane introduced an only too willing Erica, but firmly refused an invitation to join the men, pleading another appointment as she hauled her friend away at top speed, obliged to give a terse explanation to a disappointed Erica afterwards on why it had been necessary to run away from two such presentable men.

'One, actually,' corrected Jane.

'They were *both* presentable!'

'But I was running away from only one of them.'

Erica nodded sagely. 'Max Brigstock. Who, unless I'm very much mistaken, badly wanted to run after you.'

Jane was so eager to believe her friend that she lay awake all night fantasising over what would have happened if he had.

When Mrs Calvert rang Jane the following Sunday she sounded wary. 'I've seen Max this morning, darling. He said he ran into you the other night.'

'Yes, he did.'

'He asked me for your telephone number, but I said I'd have to ask your permission.'

'Oh, *Mother*!' wailed Jane like a lost child. 'Why on earth didn't you just hand it over? If you do now it'll look as if I'm *asking* him to ring me.'

'Perverse creature! Since you so obviously do want to hear from him, why the fuss?'

Jane explained, with some asperity, that Max had been able to discover her phone number from her parents any time he wished over the past couple of months. 'So nothing doing. Don't give it to him—or tell him where I live,' she added hastily, remembering her mother's talent for sophistry.

Before abandoning his Chelsea studio for good George Calvert decided that it would be a splendid idea to hold an exhibition of his latest paintings there, as a form of farewell party. The gallery would organise it all, and he, George said expansively, would buy new dresses for his ladies to mark the occasion.

Because there was a nip in the air, and the clothes she'd bought for America looked too summery, Jane took her father at his word and bought a brief little number in velvet the colour of port wine. The sleeves were long and tight, the neckline plunged steeply, the skirt was draped a little and barely brushed her knees, and she felt slightly wicked in it.

'"Wicked" is exactly the word,' said Mrs Calvert, eyeing her daughter's cleavage. 'And what on earth have you done to your hair?'

Jane's normal smooth bob had been transformed into a mass of corkscrew ringlets at an exorbitant price earlier that afternoon. 'I felt like a change. Don't you like it?' She smiled serenely, eyeing her fake ruby earrings in the mirror. 'I quite fancy myself tonight.'

'You won't be the only one,' said her father darkly, when he saw her. 'Good lord, child, no one will recognise you from the portrait.'

Jane made a face at him, and linked arms with her mother. 'Aren't you proud of your women, Mr Calvert?'

'Yes,' he said simply. 'I am.' He led them across the room to stand in front of the velvet curtain which hid one entire wall of the studio.

'What's under there?' asked Jane curiously.

'Your father's latest batch of work, including your portrait. He's keeping that under wraps until all the guests arrive,' said her mother.

The room was soon crammed with people, some of them prospective purchasers, others fellow artists and sculptors. There was also a smattering of George Calvert's former subjects, including the legal gentleman, who looked quite ordinary out of his robes, to Jane's disappointment.

She left her parents in a circle of friends and wandered off on a tour of the paintings, most of which she'd seen before at one time or another; but some were less familiar than others, particularly portraits which had been borrowed back from their sitters for the evening. Shown professionally as they were tonight, with expert grouping and lighting, all the paintings seemed to gain a new dimension. Some had the little red markers which denoted they were already sold, and Jane frowned in disappointment when she found a marker on a small watercolour new to her. Watercolour was not a favourite medium of her father's, and the delicate study of the Wyndcombe church and village pond was a rarity she would have liked for herself.

'Hello, Jane,' said a quiet voice and Jane tensed, her stomach muscles contracting at the sound of it. She turned very slowly, giving herself time to marshal a cool, impersonal smile before she came face to face with Max for only the second time since their acrimonious parting.

'Why, Max Brigstock! Hello!' she said brightly. 'What are *you* doing here?'

'Your father invited me.' There was no attempt at a smile from Max as he took in the curls and the flamboyant earrings. His eyes dropped fleetingly to the deep neckline, then returned to Jane's face, his mouth tightening visibly. He looked taut and elegant in a midnight-blue suit, his dark paisley tie perfect against the pale gold of his shirt, his face less tanned now than it had been in the summer, but still retaining the swarthy look that was so much a part of his physical impact.

'I didn't know you took such an interest in art,' she said lightly.

'There are pictures enough at Phoenix House.'

'Ah, yes. But few of them, I gather, were your own personal choice!'

Max took her arm to draw her aside, ostensibly to allow others access to the pictures; but a moment later Jane found herself backed into a dimly-lit corner, with Max's shoulders blocking her off from the rest of the room.

'I've got rid of more than half the paintings since you were there last,' he said, surprising her. 'I've kept the things I like, of course, but the majority are gone.'

'Why?' she asked curiously.

'There were too many. Now the impression is quality rather than quantity.' His smile was the one she remembered so well: wary and sardonic, the smile of their early acquaintance. 'I ripped out the fireplace in the drawing-room too. Personally,' he added laconically. 'It was a satisfyingly therapeutic exercise. Now the house is rather more as I want it, warts and all.'

'What did you do with the rejects?'

'Handed them over to the local museum.'

'Ah, I see.' Jane smiled brilliantly. 'Keeping up your reputation for philanthropy.'

'Of course. Mustn't neglect the image.' Max beckoned a waiter over and took two glasses of champagne from his tray.

Jane accepted one, challenge in her eyes as she tasted the wine. 'Not up to your standard, I'm afraid. Non-vintage and definitely not pink.'

Max's face hardened. 'Why wouldn't you let me have your telephone number?' he demanded abruptly.

Jane shrugged her velvet shoulders delicately. 'Your timing was bad.'

'You mean it was too soon after——'

'Not too soon!' she said swiftly. 'Too late.'

His jaw clenched. 'You mean there's someone else now.'

Jane's fingers tightened perilously on her glass. 'No. No one in particular,' she said carefully. 'I meant that you could have asked my mother for my telephone number any time after I came to London. But you didn't. So why bother now?'

Max moved closer, backing her against the wall. 'I had my pride, Jane. And, hard though it may be to believe, you hurt me. Badly. I needed time to lick my wounds.'

Over his shoulder Jane noticed several people looking curiously in their direction, one of whom, more disapproving than the rest, was Olivia Calvert.

'We're attracting attention,' muttered Jane uncomfortably. 'Perhaps we could discuss this another time.'

'Certainly,' he said promptly. 'When?'

Jane frowned. 'Not now. I think the owner of the gallery is about to make a speech.'

Max turned quickly, his attention diverted, and Jane let out a slow, silent breath of relief. For all her brave front she was shaking inside like a jelly, and found it hard to pay attention to the compliments the art dealer was paying her father because Max's thigh was brushing hers with apparent carelessness. Then she saw Olivia reach for the draw-cord of the curtain and pull it aside as, with an innate sense of drama, George Calvert switched on the lights which illuminated the drawings and paintings he'd kept to last as his *pièce de résistance*. There was a staccato burst of applause, and an audible ripple of reaction as George Calvert informed the gathering that the last section of his exhibition was devoted to his younger daughter Jane. He waved a hand in her direction so that every eye in the room turned to look at her in her far corner, then attention focused on the exhibits again, and Max craned his neck to peer over the heads of the crowd.

'Would you care to move nearer?' asked Jane politely.

'I'd prefer to wait until the first rush is over,' said Max, then smiled as Olivia Calvert joined them, holding out her hand.

'Hello, Max. So glad you could come.'

'I wouldn't have missed it for the world.' He took Mrs Calvert's hand in his, smiling with a warmth he had so far failed to bestow on Jane.

'George is eager for your opinion on this latest effort of his. He's rather pleased with it.' Olivia's eyes travelled from Max to Jane, and she smiled slightly. 'Jane hasn't seen the finished article yet herself, you know. George wouldn't let anyone lay eyes on it until today.'

'I'm eager to see it!' Max led them over to George Calvert, who grinned as he spotted Max, waving a hand towards the collection of drawings and paintings Jane was staring at in stunned silence.

'Well?' he demanded. 'What do you think?'

Max made no response. His eyes were fixed on the large framed painting of Jane in pride of place in the centre of the collection. Jane herself was no less riveted. The two earlier portraits were there to one side: Jane chubby at six, Jane coltish at sixteen. But she was familiar with those. This newest, adult Jane was almost a stranger. The smooth, heavy hair and tanned shoulders were familiar enough, but the face had an introspective quality, a vulnerability which made Jane uneasy to look at it. There were new hollows beneath each cheekbone, and a lustre to the downcast eyes which could almost have been a tear about to fall, a suggestion reinforced by the merest feathering of shadow beneath the lower lids.

But the biggest surprise of all was the series of charcoal drawings her father had achieved without her knowledge. There were six of them, some captured during her sunbathing sessions at the barn, others, Jane realised, clenching her hands, drawn more recently. In one she was caught dreaming at the window in her dressing-gown, cheek against the glass; in another of quite startling dejection she sat with her hands clasped round her drawn-up knees, her hair falling in a curtain to mask the face bowed over them. Only in one was she fully smiling, as she stood stretching her arms over her head after a long sitting.

George chortled at the look of accusation on Jane's face. 'I know, I know, I should have told you. But you're so damned easy to draw, chicken. I couldn't resist those sketches. They're only rough impressions——'

'More like an invasion of privacy!' she snapped, her colour high.

Olivia intervened hastily to introduce Max to Stephen Beauchamp, the owner of the gallery, quelling her daughter with a fierce eye.

'Ah, yes, Mr Brigstock,' said the art dealer. 'You allowed us to show the Wyndcombe watercolour, of course. Thank you so much.'

'That's yours?' asked Jane, turning to Max.

He nodded. 'I happened to call at Pond House when your father was painting it. I persuaded him to sell it to me. As I told you, I rely on my own taste in art these days.' He held out his hand to George Calvert. 'I congratulate you. The exhibition is a triumph—and the studies of Jane the best things you've ever done.'

'Good, aren't they?' George looked complacent.

'Pity he won't part with any of them,' said Stephen Beauchamp with regret.

'People are leaving, George,' said Olivia, and went off with her husband and Stephen Beauchamp to see off the parting guests.

'Have dinner with me,' said Max, drawing Jane aside. 'Please,' he added, with fiercely gratifying urgency.

Jane glanced down the room towards her parents. 'I'm not sure what's happening——'

Taking her indecision as consent, Max hurried her to join the others. 'Will it spoil any arrangements if I steal Jane away for an hour or two?' he asked.

'No, not at all,' Olivia assured him. 'We're dining with Stephen.'

'I'd be most happy if you'd both join us,' said the art dealer at once, but George brushed him aside in his usual cavalier fashion.

'Let 'em go.' He winked at Max. 'That dress of Jane's deserves to be seen!'

Jane's instinct was to object to being handed over like a parcel to Max. But she was still shaken by coming face to face with the melancholy her father had painted into her portrait. It worried her. She needed something to lift her spirits. And since Max was actually here in the flesh at her side again, there was no one in the world better fitted to help. She kissed her parents, then Stephen as well for good luck, and followed Max outside to the Aston Martin waiting a little distance along the street.

'Where would you like to eat?' he asked, as he held the door for her.

'You choose.'

Max laughed as he slid in beside her. 'Are you likely to stay this malleable all evening?'

'Probably not!'

Suddenly they were at ease with each other again, and Jane settled down to enjoy the evening, glad of her new dress when Max took her to a restaurant near St James's Park, where brimming glasses of Dom Perignon were supplied instantly and a large, benign waiter brought them Scallops Walewska, prepared with cheese sauce and lobster, which were the best things Jane had tasted in months. She told Max so, and he gazed at her searchingly.

'You've not been eating well?'

Jane shrugged. 'Eating, but not enjoying, I suppose.'

'It's been the same for me.' He leaned towards her. 'Since you left me, Jane, I haven't enjoyed anything very much, except work. That, at least, is always there for me.'

Abruptly the mood had altered. Max put out a hand, and Jane put hers into it, and they looked at each other very steadily for a moment or two before they returned to their meal. For a while they kept to less personal subjects: Jane's new job, the progress at Pipers Flats, the success of George Calvert's exhibition.

'I like his collection of Caribbean scenes very much,' said Max, when they reached the coffee stage. 'But the new portrait of you, Jane, is the best thing he's ever done.'

'I'm not sure I agree. I look so miserable in it.'

Max laughed a little. 'Not *miserable*, Jane! There's a subtle, haunting quality about it entirely lacking in the portraits of your sister, beautiful though they are.'

Jane's lashes dropped to hide her eyes. 'Perhaps Phillida was always happy when he painted her.'

'And you weren't?' he said very softly.

'You know very well I wasn't.' She raised candid eyes to his. 'I used the word miserable, Max, because that was the way I felt all the time Dad was finishing the portrait. I was thinking of you, mostly, and wondering why I wasn't getting over you more quickly, when so little had ever really happened between us.'

Max stood up suddenly. 'Let's get out of here.'

Jane felt bitterly disappointed as he walked her briskly back to the car. She'd wanted the evening to last longer, to tell him more about the way she felt, to apologise for the way she'd reacted to Kristin's malice. But Max seemed in a tremendous hurry to take her home, she realised in dismay. There was an intent, introspective look about his familiar profile as he concentrated on the traffic, driving as fast as speed limits allowed until they were back in Chelsea. As they turned a corner Jane's black suede purse slid from her lap and she bent to retrieve it, slithering in her seat a little as the car bumped over cobbles and came to a stop. But when she sat upright again she found that they were not outside her father's studio, as she'd thought, but in a small mews she'd never seen before.

'To coin a phrase,' she said drily, 'where am I? I thought you were taking me home.'

'I have done...*my*—home.' Max helped her out of the car. He unlocked his front door and switched on lights, then ushered her into a big, sparsely-furnished room which appeared to occupy the entire ground floor of the house.

Jane put her purse down on one of the couches grouped around the fireplace, looking about her in vain for the excesses of Phoenix House, but the white-painted walls held only a couple of watercolours unless one counted the large square mirror over the mantel. There were two or three small tables near the sofas, which were covered in coarse natural linen like the curtains, but, apart from a cushion or two, and the brown silk ropes which held back the curtains, there was no clutter or ornamentation of any kind.

'Your choice?' asked Jane, waving a hand about her.

Max stood watching her. 'Yes. Like it?'

'Love it.' Jane shot a questioning look at him. 'Have you always lived here?'

'Over the past few years. Jane——'

'Yes?' she said quickly.

'Would you like a drink?'

'Not really.'

Max stood in the middle of the room looking at her, as though having brought her here he was unsure of what to do next.

Unsure? thought Jane—Max?

Afterwards she sometimes wondered if the gap between them would have been bridged quite so quickly if fate hadn't been kind enough to intervene with a sudden gust of hail against the windows. A rumble of unseasonal thunder followed it, and with a smothered screech Jane flew into arms which opened wide to receive her, and Max crushed her to him, laughing unsteadily as she burrowed against him with total lack of inhibition.

'Sorry,' muttered Jane hoarsely against his collarbone. 'I'm an absolute ninny when it thunders—or had you forgotten?'

'I haven't forgotten the least little thing about you, Jane. Lord knows I've tried,' he added gruffly, his arms almost cracking her ribs as he rubbed his cheek against her frivolous ringlets. 'May I take it the thunder means you're not going to scratch my eyes out if I hold you like this?'

'Something like that,' muttered Jane, wriggling a little as his hand began to make downward smoothing movements over the velvet covering her spine.

'Darling,' he whispered, and her head flew back, her eyes like stars as she surprised a look of such tenderness on his face that her knees buckled.

'Say that again!' she implored.

'Darling?'

'Oh, yes!'

Max chuckled and bent to swing her up in his arms, as he had before, and Jane rubbed her cheek against his as he carried her over to one of the couches and sat down with her, deliberately recalling the halcyon time before she'd ever heard the name of Kristin Muir. He seemed to read her mind. Tipping her face up to his he looked deep into her eyes as though he meant the truth to etch itself on her brain.

'Before I kiss you, Jane—since once I start I warn you I may never stop—I'd like to make one or two things clear.'

'You don't have to,' she assured him. 'Can't we sort of go on from here? Ignore what happened before?'

'No,' he said firmly. 'I think it's important you know that one of the things I did in London, before I returned for the famous house-warming, was to make it clear to Kristin that everything was over between us. She'd been in New York most of the summer, on a commission over there. While she was away I met you.'

'Bumped into me, you mean!'

'You certainly knocked me flat, my darling.'

Jane shivered in his arms, utterly ravished by the tenderness in his voice.

'So,' continued Max, resolutely ignoring the invitation in her eyes, 'I decided to play it straight, and tell Kristin that I intended asking you to marry me.'

'Why didn't you tell me, too?' wailed Jane.

'I was going to—after the party, woman!' Max shook her slightly. 'I had the ring in my pocket and I was going to propose to you in as conventional and romantic a manner as I could possibly devise.'

Jane wriggled to sit upright on his knee. 'That was the only bit I wasn't sure of, you see.'

Max frowned. 'What do you mean?'

'I knew you were going to ask me *something*, but I wasn't sure whether it had anything to do with marriage. Whatever it was I was going to say yes, anyway, being completely besotted with you by this time——'

At which point Max's resolutions went up in smoke and he dragged her to him, kissing her until they were both dizzy. It was only when oxygen became a necessity that he forced himself to push her away a little.

'Of course it was marriage, you little idiot!' he panted. 'What else did you expect, for heaven's sake, in a place like Wyndcombe?' He slid his hands into the expensive hairdo, which was beginning to look a little the worse for wear. 'I'm not so stupid as to propose anything less than marriage to George Calvert's daughter! Your father's not exactly renowned for his peaceable nature, is he? In fact, he'd probably tear me limb from limb if he knew you were here alone with me right now!'

'Well, he doesn't,' Jane pointed out. 'I don't sleep at the studio, you know. I have a place of my own—to which my parents will assume that you've escorted me after the wining and dining bit.'

A small flame ignited in the intent, green-flecked eyes. 'Will they?' Max said softly. 'How interesting.' He recollected himself with an effort. 'To revert to Kristin——'

'*Must* we?'

'Yes!' Max drew her head down against his shoulder. 'I had my talk with Kristin as planned, and I won't pretend that she took it very well. On the other hand there had never been any question of marriage between

us. We'd never even lived together. It was just an arrangement which suited us both for a time.'

Jane was sceptical. '*You* may have felt like that, but
I don't think Kristin did. She wanted to hang on to you,
believe me.'

'Me? Or my money?'

Jane twisted round to look up into his face. 'Surely
you don't imagine that money's your main attraction?'

One straight black brow rose quizzically. 'I have very
few illusions, Jane. Kristin came down to Wyndcombe
like a wolf to the fold because she wanted Phoenix
House, and this place, too, and all my other worldly
goods. *Not* because she cherished undying love for yours
truly.'

Jane lay against him in silence for a moment, then
she broke free and got to her feet to gaze down at Max,
frowning, her colour rising at the look in the bright,
appreciative eyes which were making a leisurely journey
from her head to her stockinged feet and back again,
lingering longest at the point where the velvet ended in
a deep vee between her breasts.

'Do you think it's your money that attracts *me*, then,
Max Brigstock?'

He leaned back and clasped his hands behind his head,
grinning at her lazily. 'No. Otherwise you would hardly
have run away—and stayed away, incommunicado at
that!'

'I'm glad that's cleared up.' She scowled at him. 'Why
are you leering at me like that?'

'I can't help it. You look so different tonight. I'm used
to the well-bred Miss Calvert, remember, with her pearls
and her quiet taste in clothes, not to mention her general
air of togetherness. At the moment the only together-

ness you hint at is the kind a man and a woman achieve together in bed!'

Jane's colour deepened. 'Don't you like my dress, then?'

Max groaned and reached up to pull her down to him. 'I do, I do, but that neckline's playing havoc with my blood-pressure, and your hair looks as though you've just got up from bed.'

'I could brush it,' she offered in a smothered voice.

'What about the dress? Shouldn't it have a pin or something to hold it together in the front?' Max's lips nuzzled her ear, his hand straying to the distracting neckline.

'Perhaps I should take it off,' suggested Jane, startling Max as much as herself. His hand stilled, lying suddenly heavy on the smooth skin above her dress.

He sat up abruptly, eyeing her in surprise. 'Did you say what I think you said?'

Jane was wishing now she hadn't. She slid off his lap and began to hunt for her shoes. 'Maybe I'd better go home,' she muttered.

'No,' said Max firmly. 'At least not before we get something settled.' He slid a hand inside his jacket, producing a small leather box which opened to reveal the fiery perfection of a solitaire diamond neither too large to be ostentatious, nor too small to look insignificant on Jane's capable hand. Jane gazed at it in silence, as Max took her hand in his.

'Jane Calvert, for heaven's sake say you'll marry me!'

Jane cleared her throat, tearing her eyes away from the ring to look at his tense, waiting face. 'Tell me something first.'

'Anything!'

'Do you *love* me, Max!'

His face cleared, and he slid the ring on her finger. 'Of course I do! I think I fell in love with that snotty little girl all those years ago. I suppose I was so hostile when we first met up again this summer because I was certain Miss Jane Calvert would be bound to tell me to get lost again. But all I know now is that I love you and want you all the ways there are: lover, wife, companion, best friend, for ever and ever, as long as we both shall live.' He drew her to him, holding her close. 'Do you love *me*, Jane?'

'Can't you tell? Why do you think I looked so miserable in that portrait!' She buried her face against him. 'I'm sorry I behaved like an idiot the night of the party. I'd never experienced jealousy before, you see—it sent me crazy with the sheer agony of it. I was so jealous of Kristin, I couldn't see straight. I didn't really believe her, yet at the same time I was so horribly afraid that she was telling me the truth!'

Max smoothed her untidy hair with a gentle hand. 'Do I have your promise that you'll trust me always from this day on?'

'Yes. Cross my heart. In any case I'm not letting you out of my sight for long enough for it to be a problem!'

Max chortled. 'Very trustful! Not that I object to the arrangement.'

'Good. The only woman in your bed from now on is going to be me.'

He crushed her close. 'A state of affairs I've been dreaming of ever since you ran away from me. Could we arrange it to begin on a regular basis as soon as possible, please!'

'How about now?' said Jane, looking up at him.

The leap of flame in Max's eyes dazzled and excited her. 'You mean that?' he whispered.

'Yes.'

Max took in a deep, unsteady breath, then seized her by the hand and rushed her so rapidly up the spiral stair that Jane was dizzy by the time they arrived in a bedroom as uncluttered and comfortable as the room below, with a king-sized bed which captured Jane's attention to the exclusion of all else. With trembling hands Max peeled away the clinging velvet dress, and everything else beneath it, then swung her up in his arms and stood looking into her eyes for long seconds before he laid her on the bed. Jane sat up again immediately, eager to help Max rid himself of his own clothes, an urgency she'd never experienced in her life before dispelling any shyness. The light from the street-lamp outside shone through the thin curtains illuminating Max's body, which looked dark and muscular and utterly beautiful to Jane as he hung over her for a second before letting himself down beside her and drawing her into his arms.

He was a silent and powerful lover, letting his fingers and hands and lips speak for him as he paid worshipful tribute to every part of her body, lingering in certain secret places in a way which made her gasp and twist beneath his caresses. Jane's last coherent thought, before the final conflagration consumed her, was to marvel at her own stupidity in depriving both herself and Max of an experience so earthy and yet so sublime and fulfilling that it felt as if all of life were contained in the embrace they shared.

'I was determined to marry you, anyway,' murmured Max in Jane's ear a long time afterwards. 'Right from the beginning. Before I fell in love with you.'

'Really?' She stretched herself against him luxuriously. 'Any particular reason?'

'Several reasons. The first—the ignoble one—was that it seemed such a coup for the boy from Pipers Flats to win a prize like Miss Jane Calvert with her Verney ancestry. It gave me quite a kick to contemplate marriage with such a well-connected bride.'

'You mean you just wanted me for my pedigree?' she demanded hotly. 'Like some prize pig?'

'Exactly. I couldn't have put it better.' Max laughed and rolled over to take her face between his hands. 'After a while, of course, it didn't matter a jot who you were. I just wanted the beautiful, bright and loving girl whose pedigree was irrelevant after all. Mind you, after tonight I realise it may be a distinct advantage in one way to have you for my wife.'

'And what precisely may that be?' enquired Jane tartly, trying hard to stay still beneath his caressing hands.

'I fancy it may help me enlarge the art collection I've recently become so interested in forming, Miss Calvert.' Max grinned down into her indignant face. 'There is one picture, in particular, that I want more than any other in the world.'

'I think you'll have trouble getting the *Mona Lisa* from the Louvre—and Van Gogh's *Irises* went under the hammer a while ago!'

'Not interested. I'm referring to the masterpiece called "Jane and Jane"—why *is* it called that, by the way?'

'Dad's bit of whimsy. The book I was reading was Jane Austen's *Persuasion*.'

Max chuckled, and bit softly on her earlobe. 'Anyway, my darling, I don't see why your father shouldn't hand it over to me, since you say he gave Phillida's portrait to *her* husband.'

Jane propped herself on her elbow to look down into his softened, relaxed face, which looked years younger, the hard lines ironed out and a look of utter contentment in his eyes as he traced the line of her throat and breast with a reverent finger.

'You mean you're marrying me just to get the portrait!' She chuckled. 'A high price to pay!'

'Worth every penny—besides,' added Max Brigstock the businessman, 'it can't fail to appreciate in value. And perhaps if I save him the expense of a wedding breakfast your father will let me have the drawings he did of you as well. I want those almost as much as I do the portrait.'

'You don't want much, do you?' said Jane severely, in an attempt to hide her emotion at his words.

'Oh, but I do, you know. I not only want you for my wife but I want you at once. You might as well know now, Jane Calvert—I've no intention of giving you time to get the jitters. No dithering about with flowers and fuss and invitations. We get a special licence and do the deed in London as quickly as humanly possible, with just your family to bid us Godspeed. You won't get a chance to change your mind and leave *me* waiting at the church, I promise.'

'Fine by me.' Jane grinned. 'I don't think my mother could cope with any more hassle about weddings, anyway.' She smiled cajolingly into eyes which gleamed possessively as Max smoothed her hair from her damp forehead. 'Do I get a say in the honeymoon?'

'Since you're being admirably biddable about the wedding, I don't see why not. Where do you want to go?'

'Paris,' said Jane promptly.

'Excellent choice. No long, frustrating plane trip before we start the honeymoon.' Max grinned. 'Any particular reason for choosing Paris?'

'Don't laugh at me! It's just that I have this burning ambition to drink champagne at your namesake's—Maxim's!'

'So you shall—and if you possess a satin slipper I'll even drink my champagne out of that!' he said promptly.

'Greater love hath no man,' said Jane in admiration, then sobered at the look in his eyes.

'Many a true word said in jest,' he said, utterly failing to sound flippant, and Jane put her arms round his neck, showering kisses all over the intent, dark face, until he prevented her by capturing her mouth with his and abruptly they were on fire for each other again.

'The practical details duly settled,' said Max breathlessly, between kisses, 'let's turn to more important things.'

'Like what?'

'Well this—and this. And possibly even this . . .'

Without hesitation Jane abandoned herself blissfully to the caresses she'd been dreaming about for weeks. 'You know why I love you—really, Max?' she asked, while she still could.

'No,' he said, laying a trail of kisses down her throat. 'But I'd like you to tell me.'

'I do so like a man who gets his priorities right! And, besides,' she added breathlessly, 'I now know that Phillida was right. She said that when I found the right man the only thing I'd worry about was that the marriage might not take place, for some reason, not that it would.'

Max paused and raised his head so that he could look deep into the shining eyes gazing up into his. 'No change of heart then—ever, Jane?'

She drew his face down to hers until their lips met. 'No. You're stuck with me for good, Max Brigstock, like it or not.'

'Oh, I like it!' he assured her, and set about demonstrating to her, at considerable length, exactly how much.

Coming soon
to an easy chair near you.

FIRST CLASS is Harlequin's armchair travel plan for the incurably romantic. You'll visit a different dreamy destination every month from January through December without ever packing a bag. No jet lag, no expensive air fares and *no* lost luggage. Just First Class Harlequin Romance reading, featuring exotic settings from Tasmania to Thailand, from Egypt to Australia, and more.

FIRST CLASS romantic excursions guaranteed! Start your world tour in January. Look for the special **FIRST CLASS** destination on selected Harlequin Romance titles—there's a new one every month.

NEXT DESTINATION:
FLORENCE, ITALY

 Harlequin Books

JTR7

Back by Popular Demand

A romantic tour of America through fifty favorite Harlequin Presents® novels, each set in a different state researched by Janet and her husband, Bill. A journey of a lifetime in one cherished collection.

In June, don't miss the sultry states featured in:

Title # 9 - **FLORIDA**
         Southern Nights
    #10 - **GEORGIA**
         Night of the Cotillion

Available wherever
Harlequin books are sold.

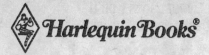

Harlequin Books®

GREAT NEWS...

HARLEQUIN UNVEILS NEW SHIPPING PLANS

For the convenience of customers, Harlequin has announced that Harlequin romances will now be available in stores at these convenient times each month*:

Harlequin Presents, American Romance, Historical, Intrigue:

> May titles: April 10
> June titles: May 8
> July titles: June 5
> August titles: July 10

Harlequin Romance, Superromance, Temptation, Regency Romance:

> May titles: April 24
> June titles: May 22
> July titles: June 19
> August titles: July 24

We hope this new schedule is convenient for you.

With only two trips each month to your local bookseller, you'll never miss any of your favorite authors!

*Please note: There may be slight variations in on-sale dates in your area due to differences in shipping and handling.

HDATES-R